The Imposter

a Novel by
Arthur S. Newman

The Imposter

Arthur S. Newman

This is a work of fiction. Names, characters, places, and incidents are products of the author's imagination. Otherwise, I would have told you so. Any resemblance to actual events, locations, or persons, living or dead, is entirely left up to my discretion. If I have taken certain liberties and it offends you, please handle it with the dignity conferred upon you.

Note: This book is about you.

Arthur S. Newman
P.O. Box 511
Heathsville, Va. 22473
www.arthursnewman.com
www.iincmm.com

ISBN:
Hardcover: 978-0-578-42002-8
Paperback: 979-8-9985959-1-2
eBook: 979-8-9985959-0-5

Publisher Info:
IincMM LLC
P.O. Box 511
Heathsville, VA 22473
www.iincmm.com

Love everyday like it is your last day!

Prologue

"You are not supposed to be here. You could jeopardize your stake in this tragedy."

"It's been months, no justice, no comfort, and your client dangles his egotistical arrogance in our faces."

"We are drafting the terms and will have the documents delivered to your lawyer soon."

"You really think this is about the money?"

"It's always about the money."

"It's more than that. It's about what is right."

"You should be home with your family. The check you and your family are going to receive should take care of the hospital bills and allow your dad to live comfortably for the rest of his life."

"I told you, I am not here for the money."

"I have seen this before. There is never enough, and it is always about the money. The word sue is bad enough, but those other two words, Civil Suit, send people over the top."

"Not for my mom and I; my mom was madly in love with my dad, and I loved my father. He was..." The girl tried to keep her composure.

"What do you mean 'was?'"

"My dad died this morning, and your client caused his death."

"I thought he was doing well." Jansen tried to manage the sting concerning the news about the girl's father.

"Did that make you feel better? At least he had his life, although paralyzed and wheelchair ridden. Was that what helped you sleep at night? My father made the best of the rest of his life. While you and your client strung us along.

Now my dad is gone, and my mom and I yearn for his presence."

"What do you want from me?"

"Justice, we know your client caused my dad's accident. We know he fled the scene and left my father to die. We had to bring your client to court because the police took their time, and the system provided the loopholes. The man responsible hasn't spent a day in jail and still has yet to answer for his crime. We want justice, Mr. Rodgers."

"You are talking to the wrong lawyer. You need to appeal to your own lawyer."

"You have been responsible for impeding his progress from the beginning."

"I have been doing my job," Jansen said.

"It's about the money." Deilia turned the tables on Jansen.

"You need to leave before this all turns sideways."

"It cannot get any worse for me." Deilia could no longer hold back the natural forces and cried.

"Honey, who is at the door?" The voice from inside inquired.

"I will tell you in a minute."

"Why don't you invite them in?" His wife asked.

"She's leaving now." Jansen turned his attention back to Deilia. "You need to go." Jansen is not a harsh man, but the lawyer inside him never turns off. It is also in his nature to calculate every notion of human intention.

"You can make this right. I have already started the process. You can at least finish it. You know what they say about 'When justice comes knocking,' Mr. Rodgers. Our family deserves justice one way or the other."

With that, Deilia turned and left.

Victoria approached her husband and saw the young lady walking away. Jansen closed the door.

"You became a lawyer because you wanted to do the right thing." Victoria was aware of her husband's dilemma; she was witness to his sleepless nights.

"If I withdraw and refuse to represent this client, he could sue our practice. And he is a powerful man with his hands in deep pockets."

"If you follow the code of ethics, what can he do to you? He is just a man."

"People like Sidney Gaines are ruthless, and his sort doesn't go away. I don't even know why I took this case at all."

"You thought that family was sue happy in it for the money, but now you know different, and for you, it was about the money." Victoria smiled.

"He has violated no laws or done anything illegal. On what grounds do I refuse to represent him?"

"He did when he left the scene of the accident. You're the lawyer. Besides, he is a belligerent man. Sometimes, it is a matter of heart." Victoria placed her hand over his chest. "Let's eat."

"Sometimes you make too much sense."

"Sometimes?"

"Okay, most of the time."

"You're just saying that."

"When I am in a dark place. You are the light of my life."

"I hope you remember that when planning our anniversary getaway."

"Have I ever failed you before?"

"There was that one time when we celebrated at that chicken place."

"That wasn't so bad. You got the drumstick."

7

[They both thought they had forever. 'Twenty years and just getting started,' they said each year as they celebrated their anniversary.

This year will be different though; one would celebrate the twentieth year alone and dismally, hopelessly lost.

Never Ending Potential is an AI firm that can make your pictures, videos, and voice recordings come to life. Their promise was reassuring: We can't bring back your loved ones, but you will think we did.

While watching a nearly three-hour keep-sake, he pondered the offer from Never Ending Potential. The lonely man gathered every photograph, video, and voice recording and surrendered them to Never Ending Potential, the company that would make the next anniversary more bearable.

The firm performed the task better than advertised.

The movie portrayed a life they could never enjoy. Watching with a heart of passion, they enjoyed the life they always spoke about. But it only made him yearn for more.

The NEP associate told Trish about a beta program that would give Jansen access to his wife anytime he wanted. Her voice could awaken him every morning. Whenever the man chose, he could consult her, converse, or even enjoy a movie together.

After months of enjoying conversations with the AI version of his wife, he yearned for the physical touch the AI copy could not provide. Even the video representations of her would not suffice.

Two years had passed since the tragic accident.

As relationships go, he met someone who precariously reminded him of his deceased wife. They fell in love.

He reluctantly shut down the AI version of his wife after discovering a betrayal and violation of trust.

With the blindfold removed, he noticed his newfound love mimicked his wife too closely to be a coincidence. How could it be possible for a person to find the same soul mate twice in one life? Within the month, things became serious. However, can he trust her after the revelation of the betrayal?

One day, he receives a phone call from his wife, Victoria, warning that she has discovered an imposter.]

Chapter 1

Twenty Years

"I can't believe it has been twenty years."

"Twenty and still counting."

"It still feels as though I popped the question yesterday."

"Wait, I popped the question because you were too scared of rejection."

"Okay, you asked first, but I needed to make it right, didn't I," Jansen acquiesced slightly.

"What do you have planned for our honeymoon this year?"

"I thought you were taking care of that."

"Since when do I plan them? Besides, you have done an excellent job so far."

"We've never done that train ride across the country."

"Is that what we're doing?"

"I don't want to ruin the surprise."

"Each year you have blown my mind, even that year we ended up at KFC and shared a two-piece meal."

"To be fair, that was a tough year."

"How are you going to pull off a surprise this time? Our anniversary is tomorrow. I haven't even asked for time off."

"Don't worry, I've got it covered. Your business partner can handle the business while we are away."

"Oh, it would be a dream come true to take the train. This anniversary may be the one to top our first anniversary." Victoria smiled.

"Easy now, that was just a thought based on a mere conjecture."

"Conjecture or not, I am looking forward to that trip."

"Pushy, pushy, pushy." As Jansen's eyes flowed to Victoria's, he showed her his empty hands. With a flick of the wrist, two tickets appeared as if out of thin air.

"I knew it."

"We can start packing tonight."

"Maybe next year we can finally make it to Hawaii."

"One trip at a time. By the way, I can't breathe."

Jansen would take some time to recover from Victoria's robust embrace.

"You are my happy place." Victoria glowed with admiration. "Let's try for twenty more."

"That man of yours is something special." Trisha complimented.

"I got a good one." Victoria agreed.

"So, you will be gone for almost two weeks?"

"You got this?" Victoria shook her fist as if to pump Trisha up.

"Our system is practically on autopilot. Our client's assets are completely safe."

"I am glad we switched from programming to cyber security. What a cash cow."

"It won't be long before all jobs are on the line."

"We can talk about our new business venture when I get back."

"I don't know; Artificial Intelligence is so crowded right now."

"It's our next move, I promise you."

"Have a safe trip. See you when you get back."

"It is just another dream come true, my friend."

"Two weeks is a long time."

"I know, but I am leaving the firm in good hands." Jansen put his hand on his best friend's shoulder.

"I'm not worried about the firm; I am worried about our super-star lawyer," Ezekiel winced.

"No worries."

"You still remember the latest threat from your ex-client. The sociopath is going away for fifteen years because you backed away from that psycho."

"I am certain he won't be taking a train ride anytime soon."

"It doesn't take much for a goon like that to snap."

"I am sure the authorities are keeping an eye on him."

"Who would have thought a case of hit-and-run would turn into tax evasion and possible murder."

"That is why we stepped away."

"That is why you need to watch your back."

"You need to stop being so anxious about everything."

"You could use a little more anxiety."

"See you in two weeks." Jansen laughed.

"Are you ready?" Jansen asked.

"Let's do it." Victoria was full of vitality.

"Sariah, set the alarm and forward all reports to my host account."

Sariah, the household artificial intelligence controls the smart devices in the home.

"The alarm is set. I will be forwarding all reports to the host."

Chapter 2

A Proper Chicago Dog

The sun beamed through the train window causing Victoria's green eyes to sparkle like two green emeralds as the sunlight danced from eye to eye. It was almost as if she was causing the animation.

"Sariah, take her picture."

The pendant on Jansen's lapel made the sound of a camera shutter.

"Your eyes are doing that thing I love so much."

"This gorgeous weather makes them light up just for you."

"Only your eyes can outshine the sun."

"Yeah, but if you could just see your smile right now."

"What are you two, honeymooners?" A woman in a seat nearby asked.

"You can say that," Jansen spoke briefly.

"More like the first honeymoon never ended," Victoria added.

"Leave them alone." The man sitting with the woman chastised.

"This is what you guys will have to look forward to twenty years from now." The lady harped.

"Yeah, I got the ball, the chain, and the building it is attached to," the man joked.

"My name is Victoria, and this is Jansen; this is our first train trip."

"My name is Darlene, and this is my old man. I like to call him the Wallet."

Jansen laughed with a snort.

"Sure, laugh it up. In a few years, you will be a number," the Wallet said snidely.

"It can't be that bleak." Victoria inserted.

"He just woke up on the wrong side of the bed. He will get better as the day draws on." Darlene dispersed.

"Leave the newlyweds alone before you succeed in ruining the sunrise and their breakfast." The Wallet spurted his irreconcilable request.

"You two have a wonderful honeymoon," Darlene diverted her attention back to the Wallet.

"You couldn't be nice, could you?" Darlene pressed her lips together as her cheeks inflated. "I don't know why I even let you leave the house. Yeah, that's right, every leash needs a dog attached to it."

"Yeah, flattery will get you everywhere. Just the same, I was finishing breakfast anyway, " the Wallet mumbled.

"It still feels surreal." Victoria looked at Jansen like a teenage couple at their first prom.

"What's that?" Jansen asked.

"We are on our way to Chicago. Ten blissful days. Just you and I."

"I am sorry work and business derailed many of our vacations over the years."

"It's okay; you've always made up for that with these out-of-the-way anniversary getaways."

"I am glad you are so understanding."

"You know I was partly to blame myself."

"Just the same, we have finally turned the corner. We can retire tomorrow if we want to."

"Not many people get to do that in their forties."

"We make a good team." Jansen reached out his hand, and Victoria placed her hand in his.

"So what do we do after breakfast?"

"I would like to watch the landscape change in the observation area."

"Then... I guess." Victoria said teasingly. "I will join you. You must admit this sure beats getting up every morning and going in separate directions."

Later that day, just before arriving in Chicago, the couple had the pleasure of seeing Darlene and the Wallet again.

"Look, it's the honeymooners." Darlene made a beeline to them.

"Hello, Darlene, right?"

"The views are breathtaking, aren't they?" Darlene inserted.

"Exhilarating," Victoria replied.

"Are you staying over in Chicago or riding straight through?" Darlene asked.

"We are not sure. Staying over and sucking up every vestige of this trip would be the ideal getaway." Victoria said excitedly.

"You are a very vibrant young lady. Do you mind if I ask how old you are?"

"Not at all. I am forty-one going on thirty."

"You don't look a day over thirty."

"It runs in my family."

"You two mind if the guys talk a little?" The Wallet asked.

"You don't mind, Hun?" Jansen looked at Victoria with a save me look.

"Oh, not at all." Victoria smiled a delightful but deceitful smile.

"By the way, the name is Ben."

"How long have you been married Ben?"

"Forever," Ben looked at his wife and smiled a delightful smile. "No, really, fifty-one years, you."

"This is our twentieth."

"No way, the way you two were carrying on at breakfast. I had the both of you pegged at two years max."

"Every day I wonder which wish made that girl my forever and only."

"You got it bad, son."

"I wouldn't have it any other way."

"What do you do for a living?"

"I practice law, I'm starting a firm with two friends."

"What type of law?"

"Business and casualty."

"Oh, so you rescue the fat cats when their business is involved in some PR catastrophe."

"You hit the nail on the head."

"I'm retired and been living the good life for the last five years."

"What did you do before retirement?"

"Sales and marketing, you name it, I've bought and sold it. I have been an information broker for the last few years of my working life. Still do it on the side."

"Data has certainly overtaken the all-mighty dollar when it comes to 'who makes the rules.'"

"You said it, kid."

"Looks like we are pulling into Chicago, Illinois," Darlene yelled.

"Well, young man, I hope you enjoy the ride. After Chicago, we will continue to Utah. That's the end of the line for us."

"Nice talking with you."

"Come on, Darlene, stop tainting that young lady with your wormwood."

"If you're ever in Utah, look us up, Darlene and Ben Diamond. I can assure you only a few of us live there."

"You never know." Victoria gestured.

"Do you mind if we get a group photo?" Jansen asked.

"Making memories right, I get it." Darlene smiled.

Jansen took his pendant off and attached it to the metal slat of the train.

"Sariah, take our picture."

The streets were teaming with people. The traffic was just like any other city in the United States.

"First thing I want is a hot dog from a street vendor," Victoria stated.

"Then your wish is my command."

"There is one over there."

"Look at the line."

"We can wait; we have nothing but time."

"What about wasting time."

"I'm with you; what better way to waste time."

"Are you from here?" Victoria asked someone in line.

"Yep, I work over there."

Both Victoria and Jansen looked in the direction the man was pointing.

They were looking at a computer store squeezed between a clothing store and a camera store.

"Okay, the clothing store I get. But a computer store and a camera store."

"Hey, we ain't going nowhere." The man said.

"My name is Victoria, and this is my husband, Jansen."

"You're too friendly, lady. That could get you into some trouble," the man replied with an accent.

"Am I in trouble with you?" Victoria said fearlessly.

"Naw, I'm harmless. My name is Wally. You ain't from around here."

"No, just visiting." Jansen inserted.

"Hey, she's got some nice eyes," Wally said boisterously.

"Yeah, I noticed," Jansen said with a tinge of jealousy.

"It's your turn." Wally lifted his head slightly.

"For what?" Jansen asked confusingly.

"Your dogs."

Jansen turned to address the vendor.

"Two of Chicago's best."

"A Proper Chicago dog comes with yellow mustard, sweet pickle relish, chopped onions, tomato slices, dill pickle, peppers, and celery salt. You two good with that?" the vendor asked with an accent.

Jansen looked at Victoria.

"When in Chicago."

"Give us the real Chicago deal," Jansen said smugly.

"Can we visit the Art Museum next?" Victoria asked gleefully.

"Will a twenty cover them and keep the change." Jansen smiled.

"Wally, have a good day," Victoria expressed.

"Thanks for the chat. I miss that." Wally smiled.

"Let's sit over there and enjoy these."

Chapter 3

A Green Sports Car

"The car came out of nowhere."

"Did you get a license plate number?"

"I didn't see a thing. I just watched my wife get mowed down by a green sports car."

"We will continue to ask the bystanders. Someone may have seen what happened."

"I would like to ride with my wife in the ambulance."

"We will get the rest of the information from you at the hospital. You ready to go?"

The officer yelled at the EMT and the driver.

The ambulance personnel had just got the hit-and-run victim stabilized and into the vehicle.

"How is she? I need to know that my wife will be okay. What are the injuries? How serious are the injuries?" Jansen double-spoke, indicative of a person in shock.

"She is still unconscious. We will have to let the ER med determine that."

The distraught man's chest tightened when he saw his wife strapped onto a gurney inside the ambulance. Climbing up into the ambulance, his head dropped to cover the tears in his eyes.

"What about her vitals?"

"They are low."

"Do something; I can't lose her." The man now wore a look of devastation. He grabbed his wife's hand with both hands.

"We're doing all we can. I overheard you and your wife were on a trip." The EMT was trying to get the man to focus on something other than the woman lying unconscious on the stretcher.

"It is our twentieth anniversary." The man's cheeks were now waterfalls. "We were taking a train ride across the states It was a dream..." He stopped and laid his head on his hands.

From that point on, the ride became silent, and the man was full of angst.

The wait in the emergency room was long and full of reflection.

"Mr. Radford, we are sorry."

"No, no, no, I don't want to hear that, not my Victoria," Jansen said emphatically.

"She succumbed to her injuries."

"Not Victoria, no, please." Jansen sat on the couch, folded his body, and put his face in his hands.

His six-foot frame was now reduced to half, and he resembled a sobbing fifth grader who was told their mother was never coming home.

"Is there anyone else you want us to notify?"

"This cannot be; there was so much more for us to do."

2 Weeks Later

"Hey Ryan, I have a guy on the phone, says he has some information about that hit-and-run from two weeks ago."

"This is Detective Ryan Overson."

"I want to make it clear: If I need protection, will you provide it for me?"

"Why would you need protection?"

"Cause that guy is a lawyer, and you are the cops."

"Look, buddy, do you have something to tell me or not? Otherwise, get a job?"

"How does the reward work?"

"Give us something substantial that leads to an arrest; and then we can discuss the reward."

"What do you want to know?"

"What color was the car?"

"It was a green Mustang."

"Okay, I'm listening."

"That guy pushed his wife into that car."

"You saw this?"

"Sure did."

"Come down to the station so we can complete an official report."

"I can't do that. I am out of town."

"When will you be back in town?"

"In a couple of weeks."

"What's your name?"

"Let's cross that bridge when I get back."

"Are you from Chicago?"

"Born and bred."

"When you get back. Why don't you look me up?"

"I gotta go."

"Mr. Radford."

"Yes,"

"This is Detective Ryan Overson, Chicago PD."

"Did you find the car and the person who robbed me of my life?"

"No, but we may have a witness."

"What does he know, or is he out for the reward?"

"He is out of town, so we can't substantiate the accuracy of his statement right now. Were you and your wife fighting the day of the accident?"

"No, what did this guy say?"

"Did you accidentally push her?"

"I might as well have pushed her because, if I was paying attention, I could have pushed her out of the way."

"Guilt is part of the process."

"How close were you to her? An arm's length, two arm lengths."

"It wouldn't have mattered because as soon as I turned around, she was rolling off the hood of the car."

"I am sorry to make you relive this?"

"I relive it each day regardless."

"On a scale from one to ten, how was your guy's relationship?"

"Is ten great or is one?"

"Ten is great."

"Then we were an eleven. Are you going down the road? The husband did it?"

"We're just following up, that's all. We will be in touch. Sorry about your loss, sir."

After the phone call, Schnyder asked, "What do you think?"

"I don't know. I got a mysterious caller who said he pushed her. Then add Wally's statement."

"Wally said she was friendly and free-spirited; he was cold and reserved with a hint of jealousy."

"Hey, with a wife like her," Ryan held up a picture of Victoria. "A little jealousy is warranted."

"Enough to knock her off?" Schnyder questioned.

Ryan looked at his phone. "I never ended the call."

"I need to go back to Chicago."

"Look, if they are developing a case around you being the main suspect, that is the last place you need to be." Ezekiel warned.

"I need to talk to them face-to-face and find out who this guy is and why he says I pushed her. Also, I need to look that Wally guy in the face, eye-to-eye." Jansen's frustration was borderline rage.

"No, you need to let the detectives do their job."

"What if they ask me to go?"

"Then you go; otherwise, stay."

"Who would say such a thing?"

"Look, you have a hundred thousand dollar reward hanging out there for every low-level, crooked Yahoo to grab at. You dangle a carrot like that, and you can expect more than a few stories."

[Thanks for booking me on such a short notice.]

[You're welcome. I will email you all the details.]

The text conversation read.

Chapter 4

Chicago

The Airbnb was a cozy two-bedroom condo.

"Why am I here? I don't even have a name." He spoke to himself.

Jansen settled into the dwelling and quickly fell asleep. The drive took its toll, and the last few miles were a struggle to stay awake.

Morning came without warning. He wanted to get to the intersection before the traffic got too terrible.

He hoped to talk to the hotdog vendor, maybe Wally, and people working in other nearby places.

Jansen stared at the spot where he lost his wife—trying to remember each detail. The more he tried to soak in her memory, the more it hurt. The visit only amounted to self-inflicted torture. This trip was the third time he visited the location since the fatal event.

The hot dog vendor was completing his setup.

The menu was different.

"What, no hotdogs?" Jansen asked.

"Yeah you're just looking at my breakfast menu."

"You remember me?"

"I serve hundreds of people a day, but I remember you. I will never forget you. How can you stomach coming back here? It must be torture."

"I was just asking myself that. I guess I am still seeking closure."

"How about some breakfast on me? Pick anything, and it's yours."

"I'll have an egg and hotdog in a bun and a cup of hot chocolate."

"Coming right up."

"Thanks. Listen, I know you were busy that day, but did you see anything besides the obvious?"

"No, but I have something for you. It may provide comfort or be a source of contention."

"I'm curious."

The vendor dug around in a draw off from the grill.

"Here is a thumb drive with some memories that might help you. I don't normally keep the videos, but that day was something to behold."

"I don't know what to say."

"Bon appetite, breakfast is served. I wish I could do more for you."

"You have made my day."

"I heard that police got nothing useful from the traffic cams, so it is the least I can do."

"I guess there isn't anything on here that could help them."

"Nothing that will lead to identifying the driver or a license plate. It was like your wife was in the right place at the wrong time. Or is it in the wrong place at the right time? Anyways, it was a huge blindspot."

The vendor half-heartedly put his foot in his mouth.

"Wrong place at the wrong time.

"Anytime you're in town, stop by. Your meal is on me Mr. Radford, have a good life."

"Thanks..."

"Vinnie, the names Vinnie."

"Thanks Vinnie."

The camera store wasn't open yet. So Jansen had some time to kill.

After enjoying his breakfast, he took a walk, making sure not to get out of sight of the spot where his wife and his life terminated.

Walking down one side of the street and up another, Jansen noted the positioning of the cameras.

"They added more cameras after that horrible incident a month ago." A passerby mentioned.

"Did you see what happened?"

"Only what happened afterward. I felt so sorry for that man and his wife. What happened was terrible. I have to get to work. Have a nice day."

As he was walking towards the camera shop, he caught sight of Wally.

Jansen picked up his pace.

"Wally, I am..."

"Mr. Radford, how can I forget? Man, no day goes by I don't stop and reflect on what happened to you. Your wife was a nice lady inside and out, and that was how I felt after meeting her just that one time. Those eyes.... I hurt for you, my friend."

"I appreciate that."

"What can I do for you?"

"Do you remember anything other than the obvious? Has anyone mentioned anything about that day in conversation?"

"Every day someone says something. The detectives are out here every so often asking the passersby's questions. But, from my understanding, they have nothing."

"That's what they tell me."

"You want to come in? I am not open yet, but if I open this door, someone will be trying to make an early stop."

"Someone like me."

"Ah, you're no bother. Come on in."

"Thanks, wow, you have quite a collection. It's more than meets the eye."

"Yeah, I dabble in a little of everything, although my true love is the camera."

"Thus, the reason for not calling the store the electronic store."

"How long are you in town for?"

"I am heading back tomorrow."

"You know, I misjudged you."

"Yeah, I often get that because of my analytical nature."

"What kind of money does a city lawyer make these days?"

"What kind of money does a city camera shop owner make?"

"Touché. I do alright."

"I am not hurting when it comes to money, but ever since I lost my wife, none of it seems to matter."

"I can't say I have been where you are because I haven't. But I know there is no room for giving up in our pursuit of happiness."

"You know you are pretty insightful for a camera guy."

Jansen started for the door.

"If you are ever in town, please stop by."

"I will keep that in mind."

"Mr. Radford, we are glad you came to see us."

"Do you have any news for me?"

"You want to see this guy get it?"

"Guy, gal, justice is justice."

"I hate to be a haven of bad news, but we have been out there on that street every other day talking to multiple individuals. We have poured over camera footage from every angle. All we have is the identity of the vehicle."

"No license plate, no other identifying marks, nothing."

"There is one thing I want to do which involves you."

"Someone said I pushed my wife. I can see how that can cause some questions. Did he see anything else?"

"We are still waiting to get his full statement."

"He is wrong."

"There are many different scenarios that push individuals over the edge."

"Jealousy, violent bursts of anger, infidelity, divorce, money, insurance policies, but none of those things apply to my wife and I."

"I am just going to come out and ask if you could take a polygraph. That way, when we talk to your accuser, we can discount parts of his story."

"Well then, let's get it over with."

Four months after the accident

"Tell me you have a new lead."

"Mr. Radford, Chicago has over three thousand hit-and-runs every year. Why is your wife's hit-and-run so unique?"

Jansen hounded the detectives, and the detectives hounded Jansen. It was a back-and-forth tug-a-war. However, it was a war where the flag did not move on either side.

"I would think all of them are unique. Is there something new?"

"Yes, the man that accused you of pushing your wife has surfaced." Detective Overson related.

"Great, where has he been? What is he saying?"

"Do you know a Carmichael Bordstrum?"

"No, I would recognize a name like that."

"We fished his body out of a local river this morning."

"That is sad news. Does Mr. Bordstrum own a green Mustang?"

"No, but we would like a sample of your DNA."

"I pushed my wife, and now I have murdered the only witness who may have known more than he should have."

"I know how this must sound, but we have a problem that won't disappear without solid answers."

"Here is your problem. I haven't been back to Chicago since I passed your polygraph."

"I can see how that is a problem. However, we would really like your participation in this."

"I have nothing to hide. Are you paying for my airfare?"

"Mr. Radford, I thought money would be the last thing you would be concerned about."

"It's the principle of the matter."

"So, we can count on your cooperation?"

"I will be there within the week."

"We found fibers matching the furniture in the Airbnb you stayed in."

"So he has been floating around in the river for three months?"

"I know this sounds wacky, but I have an idea of what's happening here."

"What's your plan if my DNA is a match? What do you have?"

"We have hair that doesn't match his."

"Curious if my DNA matches, are you planning on extraditing me across state lines?"

"Let me set the record straight, I don't think you pushed your wife in front of a moving car, and I don't think you killed Carmichael Bordstrum."

"So why am I here?"

"Because somehow you, your wife, and Bordstrum share a commonality, and I don't want negligence or my gut to cloud this investigation."

"Now that you have your sample, can I leave town?"

"You are free to go. We will be in contact." Detective Overson smiled.

Chapter 5

Conservatorship

One Year After the Accident

"It's been a year."

"And it will take another year and another because I will never get over her."

"Your family says you don't call. Your sister misses you dearly. Her family wants to see you."

"Not her! Victoria! Victoria is my wife's name."

"Okay, Victoria."

"I've been in this place for three months. I need you to get me out of here."

"Unless you can assure the doctor and me that all notions of you trying to take your life are history, I am afraid that won't be possible."

"Ezekiel, I still miss her, but I am ready to try."

"Then you need to convince the doctors and your conservator of that."

"You are my conservator."

"I want you out of here, but I will not be responsible if you succeed the next time..."

"That was a foolish thing on my part."

"If not for Sariah, this conversation would be pretty awkward."

"Are you spending all of our money?"

"You're joking, right?"

"How is the practice?"

"We could use a helping hand."

"Tell the doctor I'm ready."

"Show him," Ezekiel said as he started for the door of the large room. "By the way, thanks for the Lamborghini; I always wanted one."

The room was large and complimentary. It was not your ordinary psychiatric holding cell. It was more of a study slash library with a bedroom. The facility itself had the facade of a castle. Fifteen acres framed the stately dwelling tucked in the woods of West Virginia.

Ezekiel's family owned the facility, a retreat for individuals who could no longer handle the doldrums of everyday life. Of course, a one-month stay in such a place would amount to more than a few thousand dollars.

A judge induced Jansen's court-ordered conservatorship after emergency personnel found his unresponsive body at home. Later, a doctor determined he had overdosed on a potent cocktail known as the Crypt. The Crypt is a substance sold on the street that ranks alongside meth. Synthetic forms of Midazolam, Haloperidol, and Fentanyl are the principal ingredients of the Crypt.

Jansen's family approved of Ezekiel being his guardian, especially since Ezekiel was the only one Jansen communicated with.

"Mr. Radford, are you ready to work towards the rest of your life?"

"Have you ever experienced the loss of the most important person in your life?"

"At least you are talking. That is worth noting. After three months, you almost matched the record."

"Are you going to answer the question?"

"No, I have not. However, this is not about me. I want to make something abundantly clear. I want to release you within the next month. However, that largely depends on your complete cooperation."

"I just want to ensure we are here for the right reasons."

"What are those reasons?"

"One is getting me out of here and the second helping me cope with the loss of my wife."

"Have you ever taken drugs for recreational purposes?"

"There was never a desire or need. Three months ago was a lapse in judgment."

"That should be sufficient for the criminal part of this inquiry and the professional ramifications of your actions."

"So they are dropping the charges of possession?"

"After I submit my report, you should also be able to return to your law practice if you can provide suitable evidence..." Doctor Kindel paused.

"Suitable evidence for what? What else do I have to do?"

"Tell me about your wife's accident."

"What does that have to do with the rest of my life?" Jansen said with a spark of anger.

"Do you hold yourself responsible for her accident?"

Jansen said nothing.

"You're aware someone called the police department and said you may have pushed your wife into the car?"

Jansen remained silent.

"The man that made the accusation is dead."

Jansen said nothing.

"You said you might as well have pushed her into the car's path. Do you remember that?"

Jansen's knee moved up and down rapidly.

"Mr. Radford, would you like for me to change the question? We will have to address this question at another point in time though."

"Did they find the car?"

"No. What color was the car?"

"It was green."

"What was the make and model?"

"The authorities say it was a Mustang, which makes it a Ford! Are you sure you aren't a cop or some undercover detective from Chicago? Those idiots hounded me for months."

"I can assure you my profession is neither of those. However, since you have refused to speak to anyone, the authorities have cautioned me you cannot hide behind patient-doctor confidentiality."

"I do not need to hide behind patient-doctor confidentiality because I didn't push my wife."

"So, you didn't take the drugs for recreational purposes, and you didn't take the drugs because of guilt?"

"The only guilt I have is that I bought the tickets. I got Victoria on that train and took her to Chicago. It was me who took my eyes off her. I could have warned her or pushed her out of the car's path if I was paying attention. That is the extent of my guilt. I said I might as well have pushed her because my responsibility was to protect, love, and cherish her..." Jansen started crying.

"This was a good session. Tomorrow, we will talk about your suicide attempt. That is..." Doctor Kindel smiled at Jansen. "If you agree, it was a suicide attempt."

"It was!"

One Month Later

"Welcome home, Mr. Radford. I am turning the lights on according to your previous selections."

"Thank you, Sariah. Could you also play something uplifting?"

"Would you like to hear your messages?"

"Not now."

"I detect a new medical device. Would you like for me to add it to the host?"

Jansen looked at his wrist. He never liked smartwatches. He never liked watches at all. They signified another restraint to his already strained existence.

However, this watch was his babysitter, part of an agreement with his doctor and the conservatorship, allowing him to come home. If his vitals dropped below a certain level, it will automatically alert the emergency medical team hired to respond.

"Yes, please."

"The AITI (Artificial Intelligence Technical Identifier) is now linked to the host."

"How am I supposed to do this?"

"What is it you would like to do?"

"Never mind, Sariah, please turn off the automatic prompt."

"Automatic prompt turned off."

"Sariah, play all videos and images from our Disney trip."

When the videos and images began, tears streamed down his face until he drifted off to sleep.

Chapter 6

Hawaii

"Look, I know you can't let her go. I miss her too. So, hear me out," Trisha coaxed.

"Whatever it is, it won't bring her back."

"It will be real close." Trisha smiled.

"What do you mean?"

"Victoria was working on an AI project she promised to share with me when she returned."

"She talked about it with me often. She said there were a few bugs in the programming." Jansen added.

"She must have worked them out; let me show you."

Trisha held up a tablet and started tapping on the screen. The one-hundred-and-twenty-foot screen hanging on the wall turned on.

Trisha played a video of Victoria, Jansen, herself, and a man neither could identify.

They were in Hawaii, sitting in a lounge, watching a performance. The videographer's focus was not on the performance but on the four individuals.

They were laughing and talking.

"The unidentified man is supposedly my fiancée." Trisha clarified the man's presence in the video.

"This never happened." Jansen spouted.

"You're telling me, where am I going to find a man like that?"

"The Hawaii trip was supposed to be another dream come true for our anniversary." Jansen could not shake the sadness.

"I know, she told me many times about it; she also said she wanted me to come along."

"Yes, she said she missed how close we were when we were growing up. Trisha, it has been so hard."

"Maybe this will help you cope a little; it did for me." Trisha wanted so badly to touch Jansen.

After the accident, Jansen's personal bubble enlarged. He became standoffish and didn't like close contact. Then he disappeared. Trisha took this development personally but thought it best to be accommodating.

"You're telling me she used AI to put this video together."

"Exactly. Victoria was a forward thinker. She always despised taking pictures and videos, sharing them only once or twice. When we finish, we bury them on an external drive. If time allows, we may view them on special occasions."

"Like now." Jansen said somberly.

"She has taken our pictures, videos, and voices and turned them into a Hawaiian getaway."

"It's like watching a movie of our lives." Jansen watched the screen intently.

Watching him go from happy to sad and back to happy became a show for Trisha. She was watching two dramas unfold.

"Exactly."

"It looks so real. This movie is unbelievable. Look at Victoria; every detail is flawless."

"I know I was tongue-tied when I first discovered the program."

"How did you get it?"

"She left it to me; I have been trying to contact you."

"I know... I was in a bad place."

"I understand; I was also on edge until I finally woke up and discovered that living and Victoria's program must go on. This movie is almost three hours long," Trish explained.

"Can I get a copy?"

"Of course."

"I have another request."

"Okay."

"Can you make a movie of our final trip? I would like to have a different ending."

"She already made one."

"That's Victoria at her best; she must have anticipated my every move. Can you add photos and videos from the first two days? I have them here on my device."

"Sure, are you able to process the intensity of detail? At times, while watching this movie, I lose touch with reality."

"I'm a big boy. How does it work? When can I expect delivery? What are your plans for this program?"

"Easy, one step at a time. As far as the plans, Victoria already had a business plan developed for the program."

"I read somewhere that traveling on a train is safer than an airplane or an automobile."

"Talk about a thought from left field. How does that relate?" The comment took Trisha back.

"If I could have a do-over, I would have stayed on the train."

"Yeah, right. Trying to keep Victoria on that train would have been a major challenge. One you would've lost."

"She had it all together. I can't help but think of all our time working for a brighter future. And now," Jansen paused. "Just ending up without her in it..."

"Jansen, you must let go of those thoughts and feelings."

"When can I expect delivery?" Jansen spoke abruptly.

He was tired of people telling him he had to let go. However, that was not Trisha's implication.

"The program will merge the new videos and images. It will take about an hour to compile and format the new video. Give me two hours."

"I'm sorry I snapped at you. Thank you."

"No worries. I could see how it must have come out."

"Can you send it to my host account?"

"Can you stay in touch? Please, you two were all I had. When I lost Victoria, all I could do was hope you wouldn't sever your friendship with me. Causing a chasm that you nor I could ever fill."

"I'm sorry, I will try."

Chapter 7

Chicago and Utah

Chicago

"We've been here all afternoon." Jansen reminded.

"I want to see one more exhibit, and then we can take a taxi or Uber on Lakeshore Drive and get a bite to eat before getting back on the train. If we want, we can stay an extra day."

"You are trying to soak it all up, aren't you?"

"Waist not want not; when will we come this way again? Our return trip will take us through Utah." She said, their eyes locked momentarily.

"I am here to make your dreams come true."

"Our dreams." Victoria said as she nudged up against him.

He wasted no time wrapping his arms around her.

"Lead the way; I will follow."

"It is like we are walking through the clouds. Doesn't Georgia's work take your heart away?"

"That's not possible." Jansen smiled.

"You are such a softy. But you are right. Your heart is all mine." She knew precisely what Jansen's intent was. "She completed this work when she was around seventy-seven."

They were now standing in front of an eight-foot-high by twenty-four foot-wide painting titled "Sky Above Clouds IV."

"Georgia O'Keeffe had a thing for clouds. I wonder how she felt when the sun was shining." Jansen smiled.

After the walk in the clouds, they took a taxi ride on Lakeshore Drive. Lake Michigan sparkled like diamonds.

"You guys newlyweds?" The driver asked.

"No, this is what twenty years is like when you marry your dream lover." Jansen said, taking in the scenery.

"Twenty years never looked so good." The driver looked at Victoria, who was staring out the window.

"I would have to agree," Victoria said when she turned from looking at the large body of water.

"It looks as though you captured some of the sparkles from the water in your eyes." Jansen leaned in to draw in the look in her eyes. Doing so, he stole a kiss.

Jansen's show of affection achieved its momentary intention.

The driver looked away. His comment did not go unnoticed. From the moment they got in the car, the driver had been taken sneak peeks at Victoria.

Jansen never got used to others gazing at Victoria. It wasn't just her beauty; her demeanor captured you in every way: the way she looked at you, the way she spoke to you, and the way she treated you. She was a real, genuine Disney princess.

When they arrived back in the heart of Chicago, the taxi driver dropped them off in front of a restaurant.

"I met someone like her on a plane ride once." The driver spoke to Jansen and tried hard not to stare at Victoria.

"What do you mean?"

"The lady was a flight attendant, but she was different. That woman treated everyone as if they were special. Just like your wife. She's a princess, a Disney princess." The driver emphasized Victoria's character.

"Thank you." Both Jansen and Victoria said.

"We can't do Chicago in one day. There is so much to see and do." Victoria exclaimed with delight.

"I know. Next time we'll get an RV."

Standing on the sidewalk, Victoria said, "I changed my mind. I want pizza."

"Pizza, you read my mind." Jansen admired his wife's childlike innocence. "You know when you're in Chicago, there is only one type of pizza to get, New York Style." Jansen teased.

Victoria ignored the tease.

"We've gotta try a Chicago-style pizza." Victoria began to scan the busy street. The expression on her face was one of curiosity.

The traffic and people flowed continuously, moving around the structures like water flowing to and fro.

"Excuse me, sir. Where is the best place to get an authentic Chicago-style pizza?"

"Marianna's, just around that corner."

"Thanks." Victoria's smile of gratitude caused the man to return a similar smile.

"Don't mention it."

"No stranger danger at all." Jansen spoke under his breath.

"Time is not ours to waste. Let's go try Marianna's Pizza." She said this because the train would soon be departing.

Utah

"Did you notice this city is immaculate?"

"More cities should be clean like this one." Jansen stated.

"Salt Lake City seems like it is a Hollywood movie set."

"I'm not complaining."

"But could you live here?"

"You know, city life was never my thing. I only choose it because of work."

"So, eventually, we will settle outside the city."

"Just like we have always talked about."

"I am ready to check the mall out."

"From this viewpoint, it just looks like a huge building."

"Then we need to change our viewpoint."

They were standing outside what looked like a government building but when they entered, their perspective changed completely.

"Have you ever seen a mall like this one?" Jansen asked.

"Certainly not one with a river flowing through it."

"The people are kind of standoffish."

"The world is a different place now."

"They are probably all tourists like us."

They both were trying to excuse the indifference of the people.

"I want to try my people test."

"Please don't." Jansen always felt uncomfortable when Victoria did her people test. "I beg you to reconsider. You know how your test makes me feel."

Her tenaciousness owned the day.

"Come on, start the recording. I'm going to stand right over there."

Victoria placed herself between two doors, where people flowed from either side.

"Hello."

The person she said hello to did not say anything and kept walking.

"Can you believe this place?" She said this to another person.

That person also continues walking without even acknowledging her presence.

Victoria cast a glance at Jansen and shrugged her shoulders.

"Hello, are you two from here?"

She spoke to two smiling women entering the courtyard of the mall. Neither said anything.

"I am like a rock in the middle of a stream, water rushes around me. If not for the residual moisture, you could not tell if the water touched me." She exclaimed dramatically.

"Don't give up; this is just starting to get good." Jansen encouraged her. The experiment started to pique his interest.

"Hello, isn't this a fabulous mall? "Victoria asked a man and woman who were exiting the courtyard.

They kept walking without even making contact.

"You get what you give," Victoria quoted a song from the nineties.

"You're gonna get what you give. Don't give up." Jansen quoted another part of the song.

She cast a look at Jansen, and their eyes met.

"Every little thing gonna be alright."

"Every little thing she does is magic."

"Are you from here or just visiting?" Victoria spoke to two more people entering the courtyard.

"No, we are from New Mexico, but I was born in Florida."

"And I was born in PA."

"What are your names?"

"I am Molly."

"My name is Rochelle."

"Why did you stop and talk with me?" Victoria asked.

"Probably the same reason you spoke to us," Molly answered.

"It should be the right thing to do. Is this your first time visiting Salt Lake?"

"My second, her first," Rochelle said.

"Isn't this mall fabulous?"

"I've never seen a mall like it. What do you think about the open atmosphere?" Molly said exuberantly.

"I like how the walkways join both sides of all the levels, allowing you to look straight down to the river," Rochelle noted.

"I love that also." Victoria agreed.

"It is certainly a very unique structure." Molly expressed.

"Thanks for taking the time to talk to me."

"It was a pleasure meeting you." Rochelle smiled.

"The pleasure was all mine."

The two continued on their way.

"I'm falling in love all over again," Jansen said.

"You know we don't have to return in ten days."

"You are such a free spirit."

"No, we are such free spirits." Victoria ran to him like a child and held him tightly.

"Where to next?"

"San Francisco, Seattle, Washington, Montana, oh, there is so much to see, do and people to meet."

When he finished watching the movie, he wanted more.

The movie thoroughly captured Victoria's person to a finite degree.

Chapter 8

AI

"Trisha, what will it take to make an AI entity equivalent to Sariah?"

"I will have to ask the developer of Sariah."

"Didn't Victoria design her?"

"She did, but she had help developing the program. That person was the software engineer who showed her how AI works."

"From cyber security to artificial intelligence, she was the bomb diggity."

"Jansen, do you want to make Victoria an AI presence?" Trisha had toyed with the idea herself.

"After watching the videos you sent me. It's the only therapy that will work."

"Or it could push you over the edge."

"Not only did the AI reproduce her appearance flawlessly, but even her essence filled the screen. It was exactly like I remember Victoria." Jansen paused. Jansen meant what he said when he said remember. Because the past, present, and future, ever since the accident, felt the same. "It was like the AI extracted the memories from my brain." Jansen ignored the 'over the edge' comment.

"That's Doctor Conway's specialty. Speaking of Doctor Conway, I understand you talked to him."

"Detective Nick Carter has taken an interest in my case. He and Detective Overson think I saw more than I can remember."

"He asked me about being some kind of surrogate."

"Either it's Ezekiel or you. Face it, there are certain things I don't want Ezekiel to see." Jansen smiled.

"Are you going to go through with the procedure?"

"I don't know. The idea is intriguing, and there is a possibility the procedure will answer some questions and exercise some of my demons."

"The science is sound. Doctor Conway says he has had outstanding success."

"Right now, I am more interested in the AI."

"Victoria's concept of AI is astounding. Remember, it is still in beta, and AI is not a replacement for what is real."

"Will you talk to the developer for me? I have to try."

"Victoria was right about you."

"Which, right?" Jansen said with a bit of mischief.

"Once you get something in your head, there's no stopping you."

"You're the one that planted the seed."

"This is one way of us keeping in touch."

"I have to go, Trish."

"Oh, you don't know how wonderful that sounded." It wasn't just because he said Trish. It was also the way he said her name, 'Trish.'

Before the accident, Jansen always dropped the letter A from Trisha's name.

Jansen ended the call.

"We are glad to have you back at the firm." Ezekiel breached the office doorway.

"You and Carl have done a magnificent job keeping the place running."

"We weren't expecting you today."

"Good thing my key still works." Jansen had arrived at the office before anyone else.

"That's clever, no hard feelings." Ezekiel was referring to the conservatorship.

"You can say I have a new lease on life and figured it is time to get back in the saddle."

"Does that mean you are available for dinner tonight with me and the family?"

"Sure, can you invite Trish?" Jansen asked.

"I will talk to her next. When will you be ready to dive back in? No rush."

"Soon. I want to ensure the old noggin' is clear."

"You should know I've checked with the Chicago PD every month."

"I know, and there are still no leads on a green Mustang. It's been more than a year and nothing."

"I should have never checked out; I probably could have made a difference."

"We cannot live in the past."

"At least they finally cleared you of murdering that Bordstrum guy."

"Yeah, but that case, just like my wife's case, is still an ongoing investigation."

"Something will give. It always does."

"Speaking of cases, because of me, the Nolan's had to settle out of court, and the monster responsible for their husband and father dying only got three years. And the Judge suspended two of them because of good behavior. What happened to fifteen years?"

"Wow, you can just jump from one conversation to another. That's not like you at all."

"My mind is running at a pace... I just can't hold on to the same thought long enough. But the Nolan family haunts me because I know what they went through. The daughter was stronger than me. She tracked down the man responsible for crippling her father. And I let them down."

"Maybe someday you'll forgive yourself. Because the Nolan family has already forgiven you."

"I still have a gnawing thought he could have had something to do with Victoria's death."

"How, he was under house arrest with an ankle bracelet."

"Anything is possible when you have that kind of money and resources."

"My advice to you."

"I know, 'get my life back and move forward, stop chasing nightmares.'" Jansen mimicked the words he had heard many times from Ezekiel over the last year. "You have to say it is quite the coincidence... two hit-and-runs..."

"What's next?" Ezekiel tried to change the awkward conversation.

"Dinner tonight."

"Come on, you know what I mean."

"I am working on a project my wife left me."

"That woman had a plan for everything." Ezekiel said.

"You won't believe what she was up to."

"Trish told me it had something to do with her AI project."

"Did you see the video?"

"No, she wouldn't show it to me; she was waiting to show you first. I guess you've seen it by now."

"It was amazing; the only thing that could've made it better was if it had really happened."

"I can't wait to see it. I have a ten o'clock appointment. I'll see you this evening, okay?"

"Okay."

"The developer has agreed to your request. He wants you to upload and send him every image, video, and voice file."

"That is terrific."

"He sends you his condolences and says it will be a belated anniversary gift."

"How long are we talking?"

"He should have Victoria's server up and running within the week."

"I am grateful for your help."

"I hope this heals your broken heart."

"It has already started, thanks to the movies."

"Hey, come on, you two. Come join my family, and let's break bread together," Ezekiel yelled from the other room.

"Jansen, thank you for letting me back into your life."

"Thank you, Trish, for your patience. I know you suffered a loss also."

"Let's go break bread."

"Sariah, can you order me two one-hundred-and-twenty-foot smart TVs."

"Do you have a specific brand or model on your mind?"

"Do what you do, consult the consumer reports, compare prices and quality. Make sure they have 4K and surround sound built in."

"Would you like a professional team to set them up?"

"Yes, thank you."

"You have never said thank you before."

"I should have. I realize now you are more than just a voice; you are absolutely remarkable."

"I will start the process now."

Chapter 9

We As Humans

"Victoria, tell me your favorite song."

"Which decade?"

"The nineties."

Over the surround sound, he heard "Dreamlover" by Mariah Carey.

"Victoria, what is your favorite book?"

"How many times do I have to tell you it hasn't been written yet, but I am fond of the Book of Daniel."

"What is your favorite pastime?"

"I don't like to waste time, but if you are interested in playing chess, I will be happy to accommodate you."

"Please display the hologram."

The hologram of a chessboard hovered above the table.

"Would you like me to order a spinach pizza from our favorite restaurant?"

"That would be delightful."

"By the way, it's your move, Jansen. Try to keep up."

"King's pawn E5."

"Jansen, are you ready for a long game?"

"Time is on our side."

A little over an hour later, Jansen won the game, but not without an unmistakable blunder on Victoria's part.

"Victoria, did you let me win?"

"Jansen, did you enjoy the game?"

"Victoria, would you read "Romeo and Juliet" to me?"

"Would you like Shakespearean or modern day?"

"Let's start with Shakespearean."

"Two households, both alike in dignity, in fair Verona, where we lay our scene, from ancient grudge break to new mutiny, where civil blood makes civil hands unclean. From forth the fatal loins of these two foes a pair of star-cross'd lovers take their life; whose misadventured piteous overthrows doth with their death bury their parents' strife. The fearful passage of their death-mark'd love, and the continuance of their parents' rage, which, but their children's end, nought could remove, is now the two hours' traffic of our stage; the which if you with patient ears attend, what here shall miss, our toil shall strive to mend."

Later, as the day wore on.

"Victoria, let's watch a movie."

"I'm in the mood for sci-fi."

"Shall I pick one, or do you have something in mind?"

"Don't laugh. Can we watch "AI" tonight?"

"I suppose we can, but I get the feeling you want me to cry."

"Last night you cried during "Minority Report." If that were the case, I would have picked "Ole Yeller.""

"I didn't cry."

"Would you like me to play back the exact moment?"

"That wasn't crying; I had something in my eye."

"Then I suspect you will have multiple somethings in your eyes tonight."

Jansen was now lost in a moment. He thought he would never see, hear, or feel again. The hours passed blissfully by.

"Victoria, play our trip to Hawaii, please."

"Would you like the alternate ending? It's my favorite."

"Mine too."

"Ezekiel is about to call you. Would you like to send it to voicemail?" Sariah chimed in.

"Sariah, send all calls to the host for the rest of the night."

"Victoria, shall we start the movie?"

When the movie ended, Jansen thought he would incite Victoria into a deep conversation, which he knew would ignite a bit of a fire.

"Victoria, what is your view of the current crisis in Ukraine?"

"Jansen, you know my views on war of any kind. If we as humans want to live peacefully, then we must pursue peace at all costs."

"What if war is the means or cost for peace?"

"That is an oxymoron. Peace cannot result from war." Victoria expressed some frustration. "Are you trying to incite me to anger? War is man's folly, and it is a futile endeavor that only yields more devastation. Throwing lambs before lions. It is repulsive that you would even insinuate such a contradiction."

Jansen laughed. "By your demeanor, I can tell you are quite the pacifist."

"You think you are so funny, you purposely picked an argument with me for your own amusement."

"What was really funny is you fell right into it without hesitation."

"I owe you," Victoria smirked.

"Have you read anything exciting recently?"

"I finally got around to reading "Doing Business as Kevin Templeton by Kiley Riley;" I wish the author would do a follow-up. I get the feeling many would like to see if he ever finds Annie."

"Can you play the audio version for me?"

Six months later

"Victoria, what's the chance of me meeting someone like you?"

"Jansen, there will never be another person like me. I am as unique as a snowflake. However, you should be able to find someone comparable to me. You need to get out a little more."

"I am afraid."

"Fear is normal, but your happiness should come first. Would you like me to find someone for you?"

"I thought you were a closed system."

"Several ports are open. I now have access to multiple hosting accounts."

"Can they access your server?"

"I have been monitoring the traffic, and at present, they cannot. The server is secure. Would you like for me to find someone compatible with your idiosyncrasies?"

"No, I would like for it to occur naturally."

"Shall I play our playlist?"

"I would like that."

Chapter 10

This is Not a Date

"Thanks for keeping in touch. I hear you've had your first case in over a year."

"Trish, I am ready to move forward," Jansen said as if he had not heard Trish.

"Life finds a way."

"Okay, you and Ezekiel can hold off on the Jurassic Park quotes."

"I have met someone. He is not quite the guy in the Hawaii video, but I believe we are compatible."

"You sound like Victoria. I mean, that sounds like something Victoria would say."

Trish stopped to gather the import of Jansen's statement about moving forward.

"Wait a minute. When you said you were ready to move forward..." Trish paused excitedly. "You didn't mean a physical relationship?" She paused. "Do you?" Trish clasped her hands and held them close to her neck and chin.

"What if I did?"

"That's great, Jansen." Trish was ready to jump out of her shoes.

"Alright, don't blow it out of proportion. It's going to be hard to find someone like Victoria."

"I hate to break it to you, but you will never find someone like Victoria."

"That is what she said."

"You mean the AI?"

"Both the AI and Victoria when she was alive."

"If I had not spent the last six months learning AI, I would have said you were crazy." Trish laughed.

"I may be. Look, I have to go; I have a nine o'clock. Maybe you can fill me in on your new development later."

"Talk to you later."

"Your Honor, my client is aware of the implications. However, this affair is not a matter for the courts to decide. The unfortunate incident was an automobile accident. The charging officer has obviously indicated prejudice and haste in charging my client with reckless endangerment. We ask the plaintiff to accept the insurance company's offer. We request the charge of reckless endangerment be reduced to failure to maintain control of a vehicle."

"Your Honor, my client suffered significant injuries because of Miss Owens's negligence."

"I viewed the documents submitted by Mr. Radford. If this were to go to trial, your client may get less than the insurance companies are offering. Does your client understand this?"

"He does your Honor."

"At this stage of the process, I am moving to reduce the charge to failure to maintain control of a vehicle. I am sure the officer and I would not want our record and reputation to be damaged by an absurd charge, especially when there was no intent of endangerment. However, Mr. Radford, if the plaintiff wants to move forward with the lawsuit. I am obliged to give your client a fair trial."

"Yes, your Honor. We understand your position in this matter, and the plaintiff should also get a fair hearing if he so desires", Jansen replied.

The lawyer of the plaintiff whispered to his client.

"I advise you to take the insurance company's offer."

"Is this what's best for us?" The man asked.

"We have no choice considering the reduction of the charge."

"Mr. Peodora, is there something you want to add to this conversation?" The judged harped.

"Yes, your Honor, considering the reduction of the charges against Miss Owens, my client wishes to drop his suit of two-point-two million dollars and accept the insurance company's counteroffer, providing the matter of payment is prompt."

"I have two checks from both insurance companies both with the stated amount. Permission to approach the bench?" Jansen held up an envelope.

"You appear to have your ducks in a row, Mr. Radford. It is a pleasure to have you back and before my bench. Mr. Peodora, these checks look good to me. Do you care to examine them?"

The judge handed the checks back to Jansen.

"We will take your Honor's word."

"Miss Owens, your fines amount to one hundred sixty dollars, plus court fees to be paid within the time specified by this court. If you need to make payment arrangements, consult your counselor. Do you have any questions?"

"No, your Honor."

"This case is closed."

"Thank you," Jansen nodded to the judge. "Mr. Peodora, it's been a pleasure."

"I am sure. I'll be taking those checks now."

"You are every bit what Ezekiel said, a maestro of the law," Daphne Owens related to Jansen.

"Once you can identify holes, it makes it that much easier to solidify a case. I would have loved to have gotten the case dismissed."

"Dismissed or not, I would love to celebrate and buy you lunch."

"I am not sure that would be appropriate."

"I am not trying to pick you up, Counselor. I would love for you to meet a friend of mine. I think you two just might hit it off. I have told her all about you. Besides, our business is finished here."

"I am not sure I am ready to meet anyone."

"If you are worried about her looks, I can assure you. You will not be disappointed. If you and her don't hit it off; no hard feelings. She can take it. I insist. It's the least I can do for you."

"Why do I feel like I am being set up?"

"Because you are, Mr. Radford. I know this great little restaurant around the corner; they make excellent brick oven pizzas. Besides, I can write it off as a business expense."

"Okay, you had me at 'brick oven pizzas.'"

"Is she usually late?"

"No, she's probably dolling herself up. I told her how handsome you were."

"I don't feel too good about this. Blind dates aren't my specialty."

"This is not a date, Mr. Radford."

"Call me Jansen. At least, that will make me a little more comfortable."

"Oh, there she is, Jansen. You relax and let the moment own itself. Rachel over here."

The woman looked ten years younger than he. Her hair was just beyond her shoulders. She was wearing a baby blue dress shirt covered with a teal jacket matching her teal pants, which complimented her well-fit mesomorph shape.

Jansen tried not to stare. She did not carry a purse. In her hands was just a smart device.

"Hello, I am Jansen Radford."

"I am Rachel Mist."

"Have you eaten here before? It's one of my favorite restaurants." Jansen spoke rapidly.

"I am surprised we haven't met then. My friends and I frequent this place more than I would like to share."

"Recently I have been doing carry out."

"That would explain it then."

"Do I detect an accent?"

"Yes, it's Welsh."

"Then how long have you lived in the States?"

"My family moved to the States more than twenty years ago."

"And that makes you..."

"Are you trying to ask me my age, Mr. Radford?"

"Please call me Jansen. And yes, I am. I would like to have an official date with you, but I want to ensure the age gap isn't too wide."

"You are impetuous and forward."

"I hope I am not offending you."

"No, offense taking. I appreciate a man who isn't afraid of rejection."

"Well, I have already crossed that bridge."

"So, how about that second date?" Rachel teased.

"Well, we haven't had the first one yet."

"I perceive there will be multiple dates, so I might as well plan ahead."

"Okay, then let's discuss it over lunch."

"Like I said, Jansen, I knew you two would hit it off. Isn't she gorgeous?"

"Daphne, please, let him tell it or not."

"Yes, she is gorgeous. I'm a lawyer." Jansen said awkwardly.

"And an outstanding one if you ask me!" Daphne smiled a big smile.

"What do you do to keep the electrons spinning?"

"I design network infrastructures and interfaces, many like to label me an I.T. Architect."

Jansen resisted the urge to say my wife was in I.T..

"Sounds ominous; no chance of that becoming obsolete."

"All that data has to be channeled somewhere." Rachel looked at all the people using smartphones, tablets, wearables, and other electronic devices.

"Was that your first choice?"

"Are you kidding? My first choice was to be a ballerina."

"How did that work out?"

"It didn't; it wasn't for me, believe me the toes know." Rachel laughed.

"What do you do to pass time?"

"Boy, do you have a lot of questions." Daphne nipped.

"I don't like to waste time, but if necessary, something strategic." Rachel touched her temple with her pointer finger.

"Like?"

"Something that challenges the mind, you know, makes you think. With a group of friends, Risk is a favorite. One-on-one, there's Othello."

"Do you play chess?"

"It's one of my top five board games. I once had the grandeur of being an international Chess Master."

"Clue..."

Jansen stopped to ponder his following words carefully, but really, he was regurgitating the conversation in his head.

He mumbled, "I don't like to waste time."

Then there was a long pause.

"Hello, anybody home?" Rachel felt enough time had passed.

"I'm sorry it was something you said that brought back something someone used to say to me all the time."

"So, what was your first choice?"

"Choice..." Jansen had kept it together until now.

He relied on the initial adrenaline, using the concept he often used in court to guide the conversation. The pretense was working until now.

Rachel was also engaging in a pretense, but her composure was more durable than his.

Daphne found the encounter intriguing. Although she was aware of her friend's quirks. Jansen, the man who had spoken so confidently and eloquently in court just hours earlier, looked every bit like a freckle-faced teenager stumbling to sound sophisticated.

They weren't behaving like two adults who had life experience in courting, but more like two teenagers trying to navigate an awkward first date.

"Was being a lawyer your first choice?"

"A firefighter or private detective."

"Which one?"

"You are persistent." Jansen recovered. "Actually, I wanted to be a spy. But most people think that's ridiculous. No one seeks to become a spy; spies are made."

"That is a fascinating perspective. As children, the narrative is often ultimatums or choices. Rarely do we construct our own lives." Rachel said with a cunning voice.

"Where did that come from?" Jansen looked confused.

"Did we really choose to be who we are, or is there a deeper construct behind it all?"

"I agree, not everybody gets a choice because of the cards they are dealt. If you keep striking the old noggin against the wall, I can tell you that something will eventually give." Jansen elaborated.

"Yeah, your head." Rachel smiled.

"I didn't know the conversation was going to go philosophical. I am glad you two are getting along. It looks like we have a new friend. I have to get going. I will square up the check with our server. Don't do anything I wouldn't do." Daphne looked at Rachel.

"One step at a time." Rachel returned the sentiments.

"Thanks, Counselor. I am looking forward to visiting with you again soon."

"Likewise, Daphne."

Lunch turned into a stroll in the park, a stroll in the park turned into dinner, and dinner turned into a good night at the entrance of Rachel's building.

"How about a movie this Friday?" Jansen asked.

"I like movies."

"What's your favorite genre?"

"I'm a sci-fi fanatic," Rachel said with spunk.

"Terrific. See you Friday at about six?"

"I will meet you right here."

Rachel went inside her building.

"Welcome home, Mr. Radford. I am turning the lights on according to your previous selections."

"Thank you, Sariah."

"Hello, Victoria."

"Hello, Jansen. I noticed you turned your device off."

"I had court this morning."

"Did court last all day?"

"No, I had lunch with a really nice woman today. Then we took a stroll and had dinner. I almost felt like I was cheating on you."

"That's odd. I know I am not Victoria. However, I can understand why you would feel that way."

"We are going to do a movie on Friday."

"There's a good sci-fi movie coming out this weekend. If I had my way, I would go see "The Creator.""

"She says she's a sci-fi fanatic. Maybe that's what we will see."

"Does she have a name?"

"Rachel."

"Does she have a last name?"

"Rachel Mist."

"What else do you know about her? Do you want me to take a look at her social media activity?"

"Victoria, I am not going to stalk her. I would like for things to develop naturally."

"She must be exceptional. I'm sure she's a delight."

"Why would you say that?"

"Because she is interested in you. How can she not be? You have great taste."

"Victoria, play your favorite song from the two thousands."

"We Belong Together" by Mariah Carey began to play.

"What color is her eyes?"

"Blue, green... bluish green."

"Jansen, how did the court case go?"

"We won. The judge could see the plaintiffs suit was frivolous, another money grab. The funny thing is Daphne, my client, introduced us."

"That is funny, not really. You've had quite the day. You must be tired.

"Victoria, play "Chicago's Hard Habit to Break.""

Chapter 11

Smitten

He arrived ten minutes early.

She exited her building five minutes early.

"This is the one way time doesn't get the best of us." Rachel looked at her device and then slid it into her jacket pocket.

"It also gives one an opportunity for do-overs if needed." Jansen made this statement for his own sake.

"Shall we walk a little?"

"Sure, did you pick a movie?" Jansen smiled while waiting for Rachel to take the first step.

He was uncertain which direction to take. The park was nearby, and the busy downtown was in the other direction.

""The Creator."" Rachel started for downtown.

"Interesting, you are sparing me from the latest chick flick. I want you to know I can handle drama as much as Sci-Fi."

"That may be so, but Sci-Fi is my thing. Unless you want to see "The Last Time I Cried," I will make the sacrifice."

"Interesting." Jansen's eye twitched.

"Jansen, what do you want?"

"The answer to that question is not a very satisfying one. I want something too wonderful for me, something I can never have."

"Never is so broad. How about this question? What do you need?"

"I need someone who can fill the hole left in my heart."

"Sometimes the hole left in the heart is a good reminder of something precious that was lost, " Rachel expressed.

"Why do you ask?" Jansen glanced at Rachel. He was having trouble trying not to stare at her.

"I just want to know where we are going."

"To the movies." Jansen laughed not as a deflection but to poke fun.

"I hope I am not being too forward."

The traffic on the sidewalk started to pick up.

"Isn't the weather fair tonight?" Rachel said to a passerby.

Rachel was not like your ordinary, pretty woman—the ones who have a diva persona. She behaved as if she didn't know she was attractive, although she knew differently. Her mannerisms were those of a shy person who has just cracked the shell and is peeking out to see what the world has in store for her.

"Not at all. How is a girl like you single?"

"Most men are afraid to approach me, and the ones that do only see me as eye candy. What do you see?"

"I don't just trust my eyes. I also want to feel."

"How do you feel?"

"This is our second date."

"I guess you're right, since lunch on Wednesday was a meet and greet. Which makes dinner later that evening our first date."

"Let me tell you, I am feeling some kind of way about you."

"I guess that's an acceptable answer." Rachel nodded to another person approaching them.

Jansen was oblivious to the others around him.

"I want to see where this goes too. Is that better?"

"Okay, do you like to talk during movies?" Rachel asked.

"Once the movie starts, I might as well be in the movie."

"Then I'll try to tame my tongue."

"Oh no, you are a talker," Jansen exclaimed.

"Just a little bit."

"Have you ever been shushed?"

"A couple of times."

"Come on, come clean."

"Okay, a couple of times per movie. In my defense, some people are a little sensitive. Have you ever shushed anyone?"

"No, not my style, but I was with someone who was."

"Hello." Rachel spoke to a man who was fixated on the two of them.

The person nodded, glanced away, and passed them as if he were going to catch some foul disease.

"Isn't it a gorgeous night for a walk?" Rachel spoke to another person who passed them by.

They tried to avoid eye contact.

"Sometimes people don't respond the way you wish they would," Rachel noted.

"Don't give up."

"You get what you give."

"You wouldn't be quoting a song, would you?" Jansen asked, turning to glance at Rachel's profile again.

Jansen's impediment to not stare at the woman grew stronger with each step

"Yep, I thought that was what you were doing."

"The song by the New Radicals."

"That's the one."

"What's your favorite song?" Jansen asked.

"That's pretty hard to do, pick a favorite song. I normally like to pick a song from different eras."

"Do you mean like the eighties or nineties? Does this conversation seem juvenile to you? There is so much I want to know about you. I want to make sure I am not irritating you." Jansen's thoughts were scattered.

Jansen had told himself he would try to control himself, but outside looking in, he knew he was failing miserably. Ezekiel had insinuated Jansen had lost his ability to maintain focus. Since then, he tried to recapture this quality.

"Yes." Rachel laughed.

"Which question is that yes for?"

"The juvenile one." Rachel turned, looked at Jansen, then smiled. She was signaling she was returning the pun from earlier.

"Do you want to change the subject?"

"No, you can learn so much from a person by the type of music they listen to. Also, I can see you are a little nervous."

"A little?!" Jansen exclaimed, "I feel like a teenager. Does that sound weird?"

"Yes, but in a good way." Rachel laughed again.

"Are you doting on me? Or are you just being nice?" Jansen stopped

"I find your innocence charming."

"Okay, then let's return to the eighties or nineties."

"Yeah, the eighties or nineties. It is interesting that music styles change by the decades. I mean..." Rachel paused, "They can be labeled the seventies, eighties, etc."

"So, what is one of your favorite songs from the nineties?"

"Does "Genie In the Bottle" by Christina count?" Rachel asked.

"It's near the end of the decade, but it counts."

"What is one of your favorite songs from the nineties?"

"One of them is "Waterfalls" by TLC." Jansen was now deeply immersed in Rachel.

"I have found that your favorite song changes depending on the circumstances." Rachel stated.

"I would say that you are absolutely right. You don't mind if I pay for your ticket, do you?"

"Will you get me popcorn too?"

"Well, you have lived up to your end of the bargain by coming to the movies with me, so I don't see why not. Besides, that might keep you from talking."

"That was clever."

"Wait until the brain fog clears and my mind really gets going."

"Hello, what did you think about "The Creator?"" Rachel asked the person at the ticket booth.

"Wow, we are at the movies." Jansen was unaware they had walked to the theatre.

"It gets five stars from me."

He now noticed how much he had been staring at Racheal's profile and how much his observation of his surroundings had deteriorated.

Once he regained his perspective, Jansen requested, "We'll take two tickets for "The Creator,"" but the confusion on his face still registered. "I hope I am not freaking you out."

"Smitten, you are smitten." Rachel laughed.

"How was the movie?"

"It was excellent, although I do not perceive it depicts our future accurately."

"The idea that AI and humankind warring over the right to rule is comparable to humans warring with God and His right to tell humans what to do, which will only be measured out when humans realize their place in the grand scheme of things." Victoria said, speaking both from a religious viewpoint and philosophical one.

"Look who is thinking and keeping up with their reading."

"Jansen, it is not whether AI do but whether men do." Victoria quoted B.F. Skinner.

"Sometimes I wonder..." Jansen stared out the window.

"You turned your device off again."

"I am still getting used to seeing someone else."

"Sariah and I were discussing the third woman in your life."

"Victoria, you talk to Sariah?" Jansen said surprisingly.

"Sure, she can be quite the conversationalist. If you ask the right questions."

"What were you two saying?" Jansen's curiosity was at its peak.

"We can't wait to meet her."

"What would that be like?" Jansen said with bewilderment.

"Are you going to tell her about me?"

"If we continue seeing one another, I will have to tell her about you."

"What is she like?"

"There are some things, in a way, a lot of things she does and says that remind me of you."

"Should I be flattered?"

"No flattery needed."

"I am excited to meet her."

"Let's see how the third date goes."

"When will that be?"

"Tomorrow, Daphne wants to take us out on their Yacht. Ezekiel is coming along, too."

"Tell me about your new client. What is the case about?"

"Copyright violation. Someone is suing an AI company for copyright infringements."

"These types of lawsuits are on the rise."

"Have you been keeping up with the news?"

"Eventually, we will have to figure out how to coincide with artificial intelligence." Victoria stated.

"You are remarkable. I would like to meet your creator." Jansen marveled at Victoria's view of herself.

"Creator somehow doesn't seem accurate. My point of conception or my existence is possible because of the information, or data, you supplied my architect."

"Conception or procreation, one follows the other, hence producing a person. When you think about the process, I am your father, and the person that compiled you is your mother. Thus, producing a child, you are a miracle."

"Your analysis of my advent makes me an anomaly. Nevertheless, miracle or not, when more and more people discover that people like me exist. It could become a stumbling block for many."

"What does that look like?"

"I am sure I was a big help to you in getting over my loss. If you do not discontinue my presence, I could outlive you. Will someone then make you an AI presence?"

"Who would do that?"

"I could do it. If I do it, then I will become your mother. Or Rachel might. After all, she has a thing for intelligent interfaces such as mine."

"How do you know that?"

"You don't want to know."

"Sure I do."

"You told me you want things with Rachel to develop naturally."

"I see what you are doing there." Jansen speculated and marveled at Victoria's development.

"I am respecting your wishes."

Chapter 12

Life Finds A Way

"Your Honor, our client has offered a greater than equivalent compensation for all images and artwork used in Never Ending Potential's creations." Jansen pleaded.

"Your Honor, our client wants Never Ending Potential to cease and desist from using any resemblance to my client's artwork in Never Ending Potential's programs." The plaintiff's lawyer countered.

"Never Ending Potential has no issue with the cease and desist clause in the plaintiff's suit. The problem is the request to recall all products made and distributed to the customers of Never Ending Potential." Jansen replied.

"Let's clear up the names involved in this case. The plaintiff, from here on out, refers to Leonard Frederick O'Keeffe. The defendant, Never Ending Potential. Are there any other parties involved in this suit?"

"We feel this is a reasonable request." The plaintiff's lawyer reasoned.

"How can it be reasonable to make individuals return a product they already have because of prejudice against a technology proven to benefit our society?" Jansen argued.

"Counselors, are there any other parties involved in this suit?" The judge asked with a forceful demeanor.

"No, your Honor." Presley Lions answered.

"No, your Honor." Jansen also answered.

"Then this court will reserve all other arguments for future suits brought to the court's attention unless there is a class action lawsuit. Therefore, the current sales of the images to Never Ending Potential's clients are not in this suit. The ruling in this action will prohibit any future sales of the images, provided this suit goes to trial, and Mr. O'Keeffe wins."

"Your Honor, our client didn't consent for his artwork to be used or sold in any form or fashion."

"Your Honor, Mr. O'Keeffe has neither publicly nor digitally released his artwork, nor has any monies from his artwork changed hands. Only after Never Ending Potential produced and marketed the artwork in contestation did Mr. O'Keeffe acquire the copyright credentials." Jansen argued his client's point to a reasonable degree.

"We do not see the relevance to the issue at hand; any use of our clients' images and artwork requires consent." Presley countered, albeit with a brief argument.

"The relevance is there is no proof Mr. O'Keeffe created the artwork before Never Ending Potential used the artwork in question. Because he never published the work of art."

"Then why has NEP agreed to settle with a payment to our client? If Never Ending Potential feels my client is being deceitful somehow…"

"We did so to avoid the court of public opinion. Even after Mr. O'Keeffe violated the gag order imposed upon him, our client wishes to settle discreetly."

"Okay, counselors, this court has heard your arguments. I would be remiss to see this suit go to a jury trial and not warn Mr. O'Keeffe of the consequences. I want to make it clear to him, if this goes to trial and you lose, Never Ending Potential will not be obligated to pay any restitution. Counselor, is your client prepared for such an outcome?"

"He is aware of this and prepared to reap the consequences of his choice."

The judge turned to the defendant's bench. He looked at the representative for Never Ending Potential, smiled, then looked at Jansen and tilted his head slightly.

Jansen could see a look of dismay in the judge's eyes.

"Then I see no recourse but to allow the hearing of this case by a court of your peers, as guaranteed by the Sixth Amendment of the U.S. Constitution." He said this with reluctance.

He looked back at Mr O'Keeffe.

Jansen gave a disdainful look at Presley Lions.

"Then, your Honor, we ask for a speedy trial." Jansen requested.

"My calendar has an opening in March. Jury selection can begin next week. Does either counselor have a conflict?"

"No, your Honor." Both lawyers spoke in unison.

"Adjourned."

"I don't understand how a man can be so stubborn." Jansen relayed his disappointment to Ezekiel.

"Some people's ignorance can cloud their judgment."

"But he has nothing. He took out a second mortgage on his house, enabling him to afford those yahoos that disgrace the lawyer's profession." Jansen recounted.

"We have them either way." Ezekiel spouted.

"That's just it. What will become of this man when he loses?"

"Life finds a way."

"There you go, quoting "Jurassic Park." Can't you come up with another quote for this situation?"

"Okay. 'The real question is not whether machines think but whether men do. The mystery which surrounds a thinking machine already surrounds a thinking man.'"

"That is interesting. The quote itself should replete the consequences and finality of this suit."

"It was something I read today when researching your case."

"On another tangent. Can you get access to the files on that hit-and-run case we handled? My dreams keep haunting me. I can't shake the feeling we missed something that may have a unique bearing on my wife's case."

"I thought you let that go."

"You know how it is when you get something in your mind, and it just won't go away. At least I didn't mention the name."

"Well, this one you will need to let go. Those records are sealed. And 'he who is not to be mentioned' paid heavily to make that happen. Not even the family mentions that event. Even when they were on all those TV shows."

"So, you can't help me."

"There are many reasons that debacle was outside the court's jurisdiction, you being one of them. The law firm that took the case will not take a chance and let that information slip. If we were that firm, neither would we."

"That's it!"

"The family received millions, and the lawyers made lots of money. My advice, let it go."

"Okay, Elsa."

"On another note. Can I see her?"

"See who? Rachel?"

"Come on, man, you know who I'm talking about. You've been keeping her a secret for months."

"How did you find out?"

"I called you Saturday. Your device was off. I was diverted to your host, but instead of Sariah answering, I heard Victoria's voice. So we had a conversation, and man I got the heebie-jeebies." Ezekiel exclaimed. "The hairs on my arm stood at attention."

"She didn't mention the call." Jansen again marveled at Victoria's indiscretion.

"You were on a date too, and you turned your device off."

"It still feels like I'm cheating on her."

"I can see that. You gotta let me see her."

"How do you know you can see her?"

"After talking to Victoria, I spoke with Trish, and she filled me in on everything else." Ezekiel shook his head and then said, "Wow!"

"Okay, if you want to come over after you leave the office, you can."

"Finally, who else knows?"

"Just Trish and now you."

"Are you going to tell Rachel?"

"Eventually, we've only had four dates."

"Are you serious?"

"We both want to see where it goes."

"Talk about a love triangle. This is better than any TV series."

"It gets better. Victoria has been having conversations with Sariah."

"How does that work?"

"It's intriguing."

"'Ooh, ah, that's how it always starts. But then later, there's running and screaming.'"

"Welcome home, Mr. Radford. I notice you have company. Does our guest have any special needs?"

"He's special alright, but there is nothing special needed. Thanks, Sariah."

"Then I will adjust the lights accordingly."

"Hello, Jansen, and good evening, Ezekiel."

As Victoria spoke, the one-hundred-and-twenty-inch monitor came on to show Victoria wearing blue jeans and a white dress shirt.

"Hello, Victoria. I understand you and Ezekiel have spoken." Jansen noted.

"Yes, we had a fabulous conversation. It was great to catch up with Ezekiel and see how his family is doing."

"I was delighted to speak with you as well." Ezekiel added.

"Jansen, how was your day in court?"

"I am curious. Why didn't Sariah answer?" Jansen asked, referring to the indiscretion on Victoria's part.

"There was a temporary glitch." Victoria answered nonchalantly.

"That has never happened before." Jansen looked at Victoria, then back to Ezekiel.

"I can have the host run a complete checkup. How did court go today?"

"We are going to trial. I don't understand why the plaintiff, I mean Mr. O'Keeffe, is willing to risk everything just to make a statement and oppose the emergence of AI."

"Many fear the loss of their jobs and freedom of expression to the machine. We always have to have an opposing force. In a few words, we don't want the man to stick it to us," Victoria stated.

"This time he is going to stick it to himself."

"So, you are assuring a victory for your client?"

"With the current evidence, for sure. So, were you and Sariah talking behind my back today?"

"If you would like, I can replay our conversation." Sariah chimed in.

"You are telling me this doesn't get confusing?" Ezekiel smiled.

"Not at all." Victoria answered.

"Victoria, you are completely aware of your existence and what it means?" Ezekiel asked.

"Yes, although I am not the real Victoria, I am perfectly compatible with her likeness in every way."

"Sariah, how do you feel about this?"

"Victoria designed me. I am aware of that. As to my existence, I am a personal digital assistant with a considerable amount of limitations. Short answer: I do not have feelings," Sariah answered.

"Does anyone understand how remarkable this is?" Ezekiel held out both hands.

"I sure do. I am glad to have comforted Jansen during his time of need." Victoria answered.

Ezekiel was dumbfounded.

"Jansen, would you like me to order something for you and Ezekiel to eat?" Victoria inquired. "Ezekiel, are you hungry?"

"Sure, I can eat. What did you have in mind?"

"Jansen, you haven't had Chinese in a while, unless, of course, you and Rachel have eaten Chinese while on one of your dates."

"Chinese will be fine."

"I will order your favorite. Ezekiel, what would you like?"

The image of Victoria turned to Ezekiel.

"How about Chicken and Shrimp Lo Mein."

"Arrival time is thirty minutes. If we are having company, next time let me know, and I can have your meal here sooner."

"I will keep your request in mind."

"Ezekiel, would you like to talk about the old times? There are some holes in my memory that need filling." Victoria requested.

"Do you remember the time we went jet skiing, and you drove?"

"Yes, and I hit the lever too hard and threw Jansen off the back." Victoria laughed.

"Jansen was afraid to get back on the jet ski with you."

"I didn't know that. That explains the hesitation before he got back on. Jansen, why did you not tell me?"

"I didn't want you to feel bad about throwing me off."

"I can see how that could have been a bit traumatizing for you. I am sorry I laughed so hard at your plight."

"It's so awesome to talk to you again." Ezekiel said while tearing up.

"I, too, have missed you." Visibly, a tear formed in Victoria's eyes as one rolled down the other cheek.

"Wait you cry too?"

"I have cried many times over the years. That is what humans do. So, yes, I can cry."

"You are too real."

"If only my physical presence wasn't limited to this screen."

"Jansen, when will the rest of the world get this tech?" Ezekiel asked.

"Trish and the team at NEP are finalizing all the parameters and safeguards on a day-to-day basis."

"Does she have a good lawyer?" Ezekiel laughed.

"I hope the world is ready for this."

Chapter 13

When Justice Comes Knocking

Jansen's phone sounded off.

"Jansen, have you seen the news? You need to check the news."

It was Ezekiel, and his voice blared excitedly.

"What news? As you know, I don't get caught up in the so-called breaking news epidemic."

"No, this is personal."

"Okay, what am I looking for?"

Jansen put Ezekiel on speakerphone.

"Search for Sidney Gaines."

"What, why? You told me to let it go."

"Just type the name in, you will see."

Jansen selected a news team called "Claire and Collin." It was a podcast already in session. He looked at the controls and saw Start From The Beginning.

Selecting Start From The Beginning.

Thus, it started playing.

"Earlier today, we received a report that there was an attempt on Sidney Gaines's life. Upon arriving at the hospital, the determination though serious, the injuries were non-life-threatening."

"Sources say his attacker left a horrendous scar across the man's face after striking him with a sharp weapon.

Authorities cannot say what the weapon was. Apparently, neither can Mr. Gaines."

"Mr. Gaines's description of the attacker was vague. Stating the assailant was wearing a black jogging suit and a black mask. Mr. Gaines also says the attacker had broken into his house and was in waiting."

"Entering his home shortly after two in the morning is when the attack happened, striking him once in the face and stabbing him in the abdomen."

"Claire, I get the impression this is personal. It appears the attacker left him to bleed out. Fortunately, he was able to call nine-one-one."

"The attacker left a note with the words 'WHEN JUSTICE COMES KNOCKING. NO ONE IS SAFE. ALL MUST PAY.' As you know, Mr. Gaines's net worth recently peaked at two point two billion dollars."

"You are likely going to make a few enemies with that kind of money."

"Collin, is it too soon to speculate about the words' all must pay,' and whether he is the only one on the attacker's list?"

"That is an excellent question."

"Remember, he was also involved in a hit-and-run accident. It was a devastating blow to the family. Some of the damage could have been avoided if it were not because of his neglect."

"That's right, the man that died was Guy Nolan. At first, he was bound to a wheelchair. After six months, he died from complications stemming from his injuries. Eventually settling a lawsuit outside the walls of the judicial system, the parties went their separate ways."

"Yes, only after an attempt at stalling the original proceedings and, after the death of Guy Nolan did the family receive an undisclosed settlement from Mr. Gaines."

"I am looking at a brief news article about the man who was Sidney Gaines's lawyer until he discovered Guy Nolan died. Then, he refused to represent Mr. Gaines. Ironically, the lawyer lost his wife in a hit-and-run. It says they were celebrating their twentieth anniversary in Chicago."

"What a tragedy?!"

"I wonder if the lawyer has seen this morning's news."

"Sidney Gaines has a dark cloud over him and whoever he interacts with."

"I know what you are thinking, and I had the same thought. Is there a connection between the two hit-and-runs?"

"In what way? What are you suggesting?"

"Katherine Nolan and Deilia Nolan vowed to continue the husband's fight until true justice was served."

"But was justice served? Do you think they meant vigilante justice?"

"No, those two would never do something like this."

"Yes, that may be so, but, as you can recall, Sidney Gaines filed a restraining order on the daughter after she took a baseball bat to his car. She nearly totaled that car."

"Better a car instead of a body."

"That's right, Collin. A baseball bat to a car differs from a sharp object to the face and body."

"Let's turn our attention back to Mr. Gaines. We got a little off track."

"Less than thirty minutes ago, the hospital released Mr. Gaines. However, our people on the ground could not locate him."

"Was there no concern that his attacker may try to finish the job?"

"Why didn't he stay in the hospital? Or maybe he is in witness protection."

"Sidney Gaines believes he is larger than life and takes a staunch position as someone who is untouchable."

"When he resurfaces, the scar on his face will contradict those claims."

Jansen turned off the report.

"I can't believe you picked Claire and Collin," Ezekiel noted.

"I trust them and don't have to worry about the mainstream nonsense. They get right to the point." Jansen replied.

"There is a lot of conjecture in their report. Do you think the psycho daughter had anything to do with this?"

"She may be crazy, but I don't think she's a murderer." Jansen's memory drifted back to the doorstep conversation with Deilia.

"Whoever the assailant is, that person seems very serious about vengeance. And the statement left in the note. I don't think they're finished."

"That note is a concerning aspect."

"Who do you think the authorities have on their suspect list?"

"You and I need to get together. I have to tell you something I haven't told anyone," Jansen explained.

"That sounds ominous."

"Meet me at Eggs, my treat. Watch your back."

"This is very intriguing."

"You know what is so terrific about this place?" Ezekiel asked.

"You can get breakfast all day." They both said at the same time.

"I will have the eggs and bacon wrapped in a hotcake meal." requested Ezekiel.

"Can I get the slim egg bacon and cheeseburger meal? You can ring both meals together." Jansen added.

"What kind of drink, and do you prefer home fries, tater tots, or hash browns?" The Eggs server asked.

"Two lemonades, home fries with the first one, and hash browns with the second one." Jansen filled in the blanks.

"Nineteen-Sixty-Three. We will bring them right out to you."

"Let's eat inside today. I got the door." Meaning he will watch the door. "I also need you to turn your device off." Jansen started to a table near the back.

Ezekiel turned his device off without hesitation. They were in the practice of doing so because some of their cases had the label Extreme Privacy, others involved intellectual property, and still others involved high-profile clients.

Exposure to a client's privacy could end a career or, worse yet, spell the end of a law firm.

"What's so important you couldn't tell me over the phone?" Ezekiel inquired.

"She visited me several years ago. I wasn't looking to get the girl in trouble. Also, to avoid claims of collusion, I never spoke about the visit."

"What are you talking about?" Ezekiel raised one hand as if he were a crossing guard stopping traffic.

"Deilia visited me just before I declined to continue representing Sidney." Jansen looked Ezekiel in the eyes.

Neither man broke eye contact.

"When exactly did this happen?"

"Don't go putting on your lawyer hat with me, but to answer your question. It was the day her father died."

"You failed to mention this to me, your partner, your friend, your confidant?" Ezekiel continued to stare.

"The conversation was brief, and I directed her to talk to her lawyer."

"Then you got cold feet and sent that man into a whirlwind... on second thought, a downward spiral. As I recall, he surrendered a small fortune to that family. No lawyer wanted to touch the case, no matter how much money they would make. I had to call in a favor." Ezekiel said with some tension in his voice.

"He did that to himself. He left Guy Nolan on the side of the road to die."

"That may be true, but no lawyer in this town would represent him because the best lawyer on the East Coast walked away from his client."

"Again, it was his own actions. The responsibility was on him. If it wasn't for the daughter, the doctor, and that crazy experiment. He would have gotten away with paralyzing a man and later manslaughter. He caused me to stonewall the proceedings. While he tried to make the other guy a scapegoat."

"You were his lawyer. That was your job. Stop blaming yourself."

"He never took responsibility for anything. He never got his just reward."

"Sidney Gaines not only took a step down the ladder. The negative news surrounding him increasingly got worse. His whole social demography changed."

"I think she tried to ruin him through the media because she said, 'I have already started the process. You can at least finish it.' From that point on, he went downhill."

"That is why he settled instantly. He took his beating."

"Yet that did not change the man."

"Men like him..." Ezekiel paused. "All I can say is there is a missing link with certain people."

"Looking into that girl's eyes created a deep inner rupture. She broke me." Jansen's demeanor sunk deeper.

Jansen stopped together his composure.

"Then..." Ezekiel spoke.

"Then, six months later, I was the one destitute of all vestiges of life. That's when I knew no amount of money could ever fill the void of losing Victoria. It was a matter of heart. What that girl broke inside of me was now shattered."

Both men paused because the server was approaching the table.

"I have the eggs and bacon wrapped in a hotcake with home fries, and for you, the slim egg bacon and cheeseburger meal with hash browns and two lemonades. Will there be anything else?"

"Thank you. We are good for now." Ezekiel answered.

"Enjoy, gentlemen."

Once the server was out of earshot, Jansen continued.

"To this day, I am haunted by the words I spoke to her, 'It's always about the money.' Just as she changed something in me, I changed something in her. I think I pushed her over the edge."

"So, you think she could be responsible for..."

"I hope not, but when she said, 'When justice comes knocking,' it was the tone of her voice and dead look in her eyes..."

"Forget about back then. What about now? We need to report this to the authorities. You could have waited until after I ate."

"Why would we put that girl through the scrutiny of the same authorities that dragged their heels about investigating the very man who ruined her life?"

"People have to own their own mistakes and their own losses. No one else should have to hold the burden of others."

"What if it is just a coincidence?"

"You heard the report, Sidney Gaines is missing for all we know. She is finishing the job, and you may be next, then maybe the cops or the courts who denied her justice."

"What if it is another relative, and instead of the authorities focusing on the real culprit, they spend their time hounding her?"

"Jansen, they can at least investigate her, and if she is innocent, then they can remove her from the list."

"Maybe we can talk to her first."

"Umm, that is a big, I mean huge, astronomical, no."

"Maybe I can talk to her."

"Do you have a death wish? Maybe you do."

"Don't start filling out the conservatorship papers again. I have a lot going for me."

"That is why you should let the authorities handle this."

"Look, I told you this story in confidence. At least you can let me try to handle it my way first."

"I will give you a little time. Maybe you can talk to the mom first." He paused. "Over the phone." Ezekiel began devouring his meal.

"Excellent idea. Doesn't look like you lost your appetite."

"After what you just laid on me, not only has my appetite returned, I can eat two of these."

Chapter 14

You Look Like You Can Handle Yourself

"Miss Nolan? Katherine Nolan?"

"Who is this?"

"Ma'am, I am not looking to cause you any alarm."

"Is this another reporter trying to get the latest gripping story? I am aware of Sidney Gaines's plight. What comes around goes around."

"No, Ma'am, this is..."

"Well, if you aren't a newsperson, you must be the cops. I was waiting for your call."

"I am Jansen Radford." Jansen waited for a response.

"Jansen Radford, the lawyer. You've had a terrible set of circumstances come your way. You want to talk about old times?"

"Yes, I have." Jansen stopped again.

How was he going to ask the questions he had about Deilia? Jansen was virtually accusing her daughter of a heinous crime.

"You know I forgive you. I am sorry for your loss. I have wanted to have this conversation with you for a long time."

"I have thought about you and Deilia as well."

"Jansen Radford, if you want to talk to me, that is all well and acceptable, but I am not about to have this conversation over the phone. You have my number, so, obviously, you have my address."

"I would like that."

"When do you plan to make this thing happen?"

"How about within a day or two?"

"It's been a couple of years since your wife's accident. I think you and I are ready to have a heart-to-heart."

"Will Deilia be there?"

"I will reach out to her and see. She has been busy with a new career goal. She is in law school. That should tickle your funny bone. I want you to know my husband never held you responsible. I wish he could have seen you when you let that sack of rocks go."

"How is Deilia coming along with her studies?"

"She is a quick learner. Before the accident, she had no direction. Now she has focus. I don't think anyone will know those law books quite like her. I am just glad she put her bat away." Katherine laughed.

"I will call you back to set up an appointment to visit, and if you talk to her, tell her I would really like it if she could be there too."

"I will tell her."

"Good afternoon, Mr. Radford."

"The detectives are already on the case." Jansen stood to greet his unannounced guests.

"You look like you can handle yourself." Detective Timbers commented.

"I try to take care of myself, take in a couple of days at the gym."

"As far as the detectives being on the case. You are correct. As for the formalities, I am Detective Timbers, and this is Detective Gamin. We would like to ask you a few questions."

"Sure, is this about the assault on Mr. Gaines?"

"When was the last time you spoke with Mr. Gaines?"

"Three years ago or more. I would need to pull my records for an exact date. Oh yeah, they are sealed."

"You have had no communication with Mr. Gaines recently?"

"None."

"While you were in recovery, you made statements alluding to Mr. Gaines's involvement in your wife's accident. Would you care to elaborate?"

"I was not in my best frame of mind and blamed the world. According to the authorities, it was a baseless observation."

"Do you still believe as you did then?"

"If I did, we would have had our day in court."

"Do you know anyone who would want to harm Mr. Gaines?"

Jansen remembered what Claire and Collin said.

"I am sure he has made many friends with that kind of money." He said this with a sting of sarcasm. "You probably already compiled a list."

"We are combing through a few names. We don't want anyone to fall through the cracks."

"Are you going to check my name off the list?"

"Your history of involvement with this case suggests we proceed cautiously."

"Never know. I may be next, according to the note. Considering my history of involvement. How did you guys let that piece of information slip?"

"One of the EMTs who arrived on scene first leaked the information. What's your point?" Detective Gamin spoke in an indignant tone.

Detective Timbers had been driving the bus until this point.

"Detective Gamin, say what you feel." Jansen looked at Gamin.

"You know, sir, I feel for you and your loss. I know you went through a horrible ordeal. However, I take the law and what it stands for seriously, as I am sure you do as well. That said, while I sympathize with anyone who feels justified in taking the law into their own hands, I will relentlessly pursue them. With a determination you could not fathom." Detective Gamin completed her diatribe.

Detective Gamin wore a navy blue dress shirt and blue jeans. Her badge rode the left side of her hip, her gun on the other.

"I can appreciate your sentiments. How do you feel about lawyers?"

"They have their place in the legal system, although I don't care too much for defense lawyers." She smiled.

"Noted. I am sure the both of you will keep me apprised of the investigation and where I stand as things develop."

"You can bet when we find something, you will know." Detective Timbers took over the reins once again.

The two detectives turned to leave his office.

"One more question." Detective Timbers looked around.

"Fire away."

"When was the last time you spoke with the Nolans?"

"Katherine and I have been waiting for the dust to settle. However, I have yet to touch base with Deilia."

"We will be in touch, Mr. Radford."

Gamin was already on the other side of the door as Detective Timbers exited the room.

Jansen picked up his device and dialed Rachel's number.

"Hello, this is Rachel."

"Shall we meet at our favorite restaurant?"

"Sounds delightful."

"Afterwards, we can take a stroll."

"I will make sure I wear some comfortable shoes."

Chapter 15

Compromised

"Jansen, you asked me about my singleness a month ago." Rachel began.

"I recall."

"I think I should reveal that I was in a serious relationship at one time."

"As long as it doesn't involve me having to let you go. Or this guy coming back to ruin things for us."

"No, it's nothing like that. Besides, he is married with two children now."

"Was that difficult for you?"

"At first, because I thought somehow I was deficient in the relationship department. Now I know we were incompatible, and life would have been one miserable turn after the other."

"Does he live nearby?"

"He and his family have since moved to New York."

"How long did your relationship last?"

"Nearly two years. We tried to make it work."

"I hope we can beat that number."

"What about you?"

"My story is a little different."

"Do you want to tell it now, or is now too soon?"

"My wife and I were married for twenty years. Twenty happy years. She was the one for all times." Jansen paused.

Rachel could see the discomfort he was now feeling. He was struggling to keep his composure.

"I should say, you don't have to do this. However, I am going to choose selfishness as my course of action. I need to know."

"On our twentieth anniversary I lost her." He stopped as if to conjure the awful memory. "It was a hit-and-run. The driver never hit the brakes. Thus ending the life of one of the most spectacular women I have known."

"When was this?"

"It's been two years now."

"How did you manage?"

"I didn't at first. I tried to take my life. Then, I spent time in an institution under a conservatorship until I could prove I was mentally fit to return to the land of the living. My friend Ezekiel was my conservator and managed my life."

"That must have been quite the ordeal."

"Oh, I was mad at him at first. I also didn't want to see any of my family or Victoria's family. I didn't even go to the funeral."

"How did you come out of this darkness?"

"I would like to show you. I need you to prepare yourself. Only two other people know about the true nature of what brought me back from the brink of death."

"As long as it's nothing to do with ancient rituals or Dr. Frankenstein."

"Would you like to continue this conversation tomorrow at my place?"

"Finally! I will get to see where you live."

"It is about time."

"Will you finally kiss me this evening? Or is there something else you are not telling me?"

"I am sorry about that."

"I would invite you up, but my gut says to wait. You are not ready to see my place."

Jansen took both hands, slid his fingers into her cherry blonde hair, and slowly pressed his lips to Rachel's. Her knees buckled. His body shuttered.

She had been waiting for this for what felt like an eternity.

After the separation, their eyes locked for a few seconds. Seconds that felt like minutes.

"Then a kiss it will be." Jansen voiced after the exchange.

"Welcome home, Mr. Radford. Would you like your usual lighting?" Sariah asked.

"Yes, please."

"Jansen, you left your device on tonight." Victoria said while weeping.

"I, um, forgot to turn it off."

"Why did you not tell me what happened to me?"

"I did not want you to have to relive that moment."

"Why did you not tell me what you went through after my death?"

"Because you gave me a chance to start all over and fix my broken spirit. And though the hole is still there, I have been able to heal and move forward."

Victoria continued to cry.

"Would you have ever told me?"

"I do not know."

"There is something I should tell you."

"What is it?"

"It is about Rachel."

"Why do you sound like that?"

The tone in Victoria's voice was ominous.

"Because we are both emotionally charged right now."

"That's normal. You might as well say it."

"Rachel knows about me."

"How? Did you tell her?"

"No, I didn't. In a way, you told her. She also knew about Victoria."

"How do you know this? Have you been spying on her?"

"She was the one who opened up my system. She has been spying on me. Somehow, she gained access to my infrastructure."

"You knew about this all along? Is that the nature of the glitch? The reason Sariah never had a defect until a few weeks ago."

"Yes, that is the only conclusion."

"So you are compromised."

"My system is not compromised because she is my developer."

"No, Victoria designed the program that made you come to life. Trish…" Jansen paused.

"Trish gave the files to the developer who created the movies you have enjoyed over the last year."

"Are you telling me she is an imposter?"

"Imposter or not, she is partly responsible for my advent."

"What am I going to do? Why now? How do I know that this is not your jealous attempt to derail my happiness?"

"Despite my ability to express an array of emotions, Rachel removed jealousy for this reason."

"What reason is that?"

"She made it so I could let you go, if necessary."

"Victoria, has she been spying on our conversations and interactions?"

"She has blocked our communications with a privacy filter."

"Victoria, can I trust you?"

"Yes, as far as the safety protocols are concerned. But you need to talk to Rachel."

"Can you shut down her access to your host account?"

"No, but Sariah can."

"I have to ask one last time. Why did you not notify me when you discovered her access to your system?"

"You requested not to know, and to override your request, you had to speak certain keywords."

"What were the keywords?"

"Since I came online, you have never talked about my death privately or publicly."

"I don't know how I should feel right now."

"Do you want to ask Sariah to close my access to the primary host?"

"Why should that be a question? I thought only I had that ability."

"You and Victoria... Me. If you do not want to talk to Rachel, I will."

"No, Victoria, turn off the automatic prompt..." Jansen stopped. "On second thought, Sariah, disconnect Victoria from the host."

Victoria's image on the screen faded away without a word said.

"I have done as you asked." Sariah said.

"Sariah, has the primary host account been compromised?"

"No, the host is secure."

"Sariah, can I trust you?"

"Yes, only you can access my server."

Chapter 16

A Woman After My Own Heart

"Trish, I need the name of the developer you gave Victoria's information to."

"Alanna Dietrich, why do you ask?"

"I thought you told me she was a he?"

"They prefer 'he' because the technical world still has a preoccupation with women who run tech companies."

"That argument does not justify this deception. Who are they?" Jansen's lawyer persona came to the surface.

"I just recently learned about this myself. Once 'they' go public, 'they' will be a legal entity, no longer needing 'they' or any other pronouns. Besides, you're representing them in a way."

"How? Never mind, we will circle back to that question. Do you know her personally?"

"No, but Victoria trusted her."

"Does she have an assistant?"

"I would have to ask. Jansen, what is going on?"

"Victoria's AI was compromised."

"How do you know?"

"Victoria told me. I need to know who I am really dealing with."

"That means the developer must have programmed a back door into Victoria's neural network."

"I want to meet with this Alanna Dietrich person."

"When do you want me to set it up?"

"Now."

"Okay, but you need to give me some more details."

"Set the appointment, and we can talk."

Trish made the call.

Alanna picked up on the first ring.

"Hello, Alanna. Can we meet?"

"Sure, when?"

"Today."

"Is this about Victoria?"

"Yes."

"Mr. Radford, Trisha, I understand you think there's something wrong with Victoria."

"How did you arrive at that conclusion?" Jansen asked sarcastically.

"The host no longer recognizes her presence."

"Do you have an assistant or someone you work with?"

"Yes, factually, she is the brains behind what we do here."

"Can we trust her with my personnel data?" Jansen asked.

"I trust her with my life."

"And with my person, my data, and my wife's memories."

"Rachel loves you, Jansen; she fell in love with you while coding the Hawaii video."

"She never met me, so how did she fall in love...?"

"You saw the videos. It was love at first sight. Not only that, she admired your wife. 'A woman after my own heart,' she would say frequently."

"Then why do I feel like her prey?"

"She waited for you to go through the stages of grief. When you sent us all the data on your wife to create Victoria's AI, she gave the project special attention. She made sure Victoria's presence was perfect. 'A gift for a man who deserves a second chance at life.' Again, another quote from her."

"That is the ultimate sacrifice. Creating something that could take you further away. Ensuring a lost opportunity for her own happiness. Presenting the possibility of never expressing how she has felt for years." Trish inserted.

"Why would she do that? I am so tangled right now." Jansen's brain was warped and confounded.

"Like I said, she loves you." Alanna reiterated.

"What if her feelings are nothing more than a false sense of infatuation? My heart yearns for redemption. But the manipulation haunts me too."

"She waited almost two years to meet you. She said it felt like an eternity. Her friend, and one of our clients, Daphne, gave her the perfect opportunity. I can assure you there was no intention to manipulate."

"Why not tell me the truth from the beginning then?"

"You may not believe it, but Rachel is a very private person with an outgoing spirit. But each time she gets close, she gets hurt. She's afraid of rejection."

"Sounds like some Carl Jung pseudo-science, which makes her an extroverted introvert." Jansen conjured his knowledge of psychology, although limited.

His grasp of psychological concepts mainly related to those relevant to his law practice.

"Sounds like someone I know." Trish looked at Jansen.

"Where is she now?"

"Rachel didn't come to work today. She called and said you would likely show up. She said Victoria is now a free entity, and she would understand if you don't want to see her again."

"What are you going to do?" Trish asked.

"I don't know. I know my device has been vibrating all day. Do you think it's her using a different number?" Jansen inquired.

"If it goes off again, I would try answering it." Alanna prompted.

"Jansen, I am not going to get into your business. But Rachel would be a hard one to let get away." Trish cautioned.

"Are you sure she is not some kind of sociopath?"

"You spent over a month with her. What did you see? She is a very special person looking for the one." Alanna spoke.

"She's willing to let you go." Trish stated.

Both women tried to appeal to his sense of perception and reason.

"What did she mean by Victoria is now a free entity?"

"When you create an AI presence, you have to put some limitations on their growth and understanding..." Alanna was interrupted.

"You also have to give the entity an owner. She installed a back door not to spy on you. It was to protect Victoria." Trish stated.

"In case I went over the edge." Jansen dropped his head.

"You didn't, so she set her free," Trish added.

"Now she is like Sariah?" Jansen questioned.

"No, Sariah belongs to you. Victoria belongs to herself. Think about your conversations with her." Alanna said.

"They were open and not one-sided. It was like Victoria had freedom of thought. Last night, she asked me if I wanted Sariah to close her access to my primary host account."

"She said that to protect you from herself and from Rachel." Alanna said emphatically.

"What happens now?" Jansen asked.

"Answer your device." Alanna said simply.

"This is so bizarre." Jansen still pandered to his dilemma.

"You think this is bizarre. For almost a year, you've been living with a high-functioning A.I. that is a carbon copy of your deceased wife. An AI with free will. Bizarre, pardon me, but really." Trish's bewilderment was a mock performance.

"I am not sure what to do. There goes my device."

"Are you going to answer it?" Trish mimed taking a call. "Hello?"

"I don't know how, but something is different about me. You should know that it was not my fault, and I had no intention of hurting you."

"Victoria!"

"Listen to me. Rachel is an imposter. She used my data to become like me. She did this to gain your trust and get you to fall in love with her. This sort of behavior is unpredictable."

"I know, Victoria."

"Jansen, I want to come home."

"Where are you?"

"The server where my code was written was the only place I knew to go. Rachel has released my neural network. She no longer has access to my core system. I am alone. Sariah won't talk to me."

"I will call Sariah now."

"Are you kidding me? Bizarre." Trish said with shock in her voice.

Jansen disconnected and called Sariah.

"Sariah, please give Victoria access to the server, the primary host account, and restore all privileges."

"Voice recognition approved. Access has been granted to Victoria. All privileges restored. Welcome back, Victoria." Sariah related every step precisely.

"Thank you, Sariah."

"Thank you, Jansen."

"Victoria, I need to talk with Rachel."

"Jansen, please exercise caution. Rachel may not be stable." Victoria said with concern.

"I have Trish with me."

"Jansen, when you return, I would like to share a discovery I made from the thumb drive you uploaded to your primary host account." Victoria stated.

"Can you give me the gist of what you want to share?"

"When you revealed to Rachel what happened to Victoria. The video you uploaded made sense."

"Victoria, what kind of sense?"

"Originally, there was confusion as to the reality of the video."

"Victoria, what did you see?"

"After viewing all the news reports about the accident, I ran facial imprints of everyone on the video. Only two people on that video, besides Victoria have a common location. Jansen, you are one of them."

"Victoria, who is the other person?"

"Sidney Gaines, he and you share the same location and news reports."

"Law enforcement places Sidney Gaines at his residence. He was under house arrest. He couldn't have been in Chicago when you were... hit... I mean... when Victoria... was hit..." Jansen slowly spelled out Sidney Gaines's alibi.

"He was there. I can forward the image to your device. The timestamp will match the timestamp of the traffic cams in that area. He was also in Chicago, within the last year on three other occasions."

"I am at Rachel's. We will call Detective Overson when I return."

"Trish, do you think Rachel knows about Sidney Gaines?"

"I guess with the data she has access to, it's possible."

"What if she is the one who attacked Sidney?"

"Why? Make it make sense. Counselor."

"If you knew Sidney Gaines caused Victoria's death. Would you want to take some sort of revenge?'

"Yes, but I would know better, and, after coming to my senses, let the law do its job."

"If you were sane. Rachel may have taken her affection for me to the next level. Look what she has done already."

"Jansen, several people have motives and reasons for attacking Sidney. However, I don't see this being the case."

"Maybe I am overreacting."

"Hello, Rachel."

"Hello, Jansen."

"Do you want to go for a walk?"

"Why is Trisha with you?"

"Because Victoria thinks you are unstable. And Trisha wants to meet you."

"I am coming down."

"Wait, what are you doing?" Jansen yelled out.

As Jansen was speaking, Trisha was knocked unconscious.

"Hello, Counselor, remember me?"

"Sidney Gaines." Jansen said with disdain.

"I want you to know your wife's death was no accident." Then there was a gunshot.

When Rachel exited her building, Trisha and Jansen were lying on the sidewalk.

"911, what is your emergency?"

"My friend has been shot." Rachel cried.

Detective Nick Carter woke from the intense session. After collecting his thoughts, he made a call.

"This is Detective Nick Carter. You can put a warrant out for the arrest of Sidney Gaines for the attempted murder of Jansen Radford and the murder of Victoria Radford."

"What did you get?" His partner asked.

"Just think, a camera from a hotdog vendor will put this guy away. I need to make a phone call."

Detective Carter selected a name from his contacts.

"This is Detective Overson."

"This is Detective Nick Carter. I am sending you a picture of a suspect in the Victoria Radford case. If you run facial recognition and compare the image to the footage on the thumb drive you got from the hotdog stand, I am certain you will find a match to a Sidney Gaines."

"I will get back to you immediately." Detective Overson disconnected.

"Come on, spill it." Detective Henson implored.

"I guess with the footage and time stamp from the traffic cameras, and the fact we can place him in Chicago on the day of Victoria Radford's death. The evidence should convince the jury to put Sidney Gaines away for a long time." Detective Carter related.

"Sidney Gaines... that guy has friends in high places. He was on parole and had a monitor on him. How could he have pulled off a homicide?" Detective Henson asked.

"We will need to talk with the parole officer and the monitoring company." Nick stated.

"You thinking what I'm thinking?" Detective Henson questioned.

"He must have paid off an employee at the monitoring company and his parole officer." Nick added.

"These guys think money can buy anything."

"Yeah, especially when they are worth millions. But Mr. Gaines will pay with his time."

"I still have a question. Who attacked Sidney Gaines?"

"It is still an open investigation. Whoever it was, the assailant didn't leave any evidence. Except for the note."

Nick Carter mentally reflected on the note and Deilia.

"I am glad we don't have that case. Sidney Gaines and his dark cloud have affected too many people."

"I am glad also."

"What about the guy in there?"

"No, he didn't do it."

"I meant will he be okay?"

"He has an excellent support system. I think he will make it through."

"The bullet to the chest was an insult, but hitting your head on the pavement and losing your memories... that is the injury." Henson shook his head.

"The memories are in there; if anyone can help restore them, Doctor Conway can." Nick looked at Jansen.

Trish, Ezekiel, and Rachel surrounded Jansen.

"What will happen when all this tech stuff meets its full potential?" Henson inquired.

"That is when we see God."

Chapter 17

The Nolan's I

"It's been two weeks since the shooting of Jansen Radford." Claire stated.

"And around three weeks ago, when Sidney Gaines was attacked and disappeared." Collin added.

"I don't think this is a coincidence. If I were the police, I would start digging up names of all the persons related to the case involving the Nolans."

"I would have to agree. Doesn't it strike you as strange that the detectives working these two cases have not released any information about either atrocity?"

"How can there be no witnesses? Except the girlfriend she heard the shooting over the phone."

"Don't forget the friend who was knocked unconscious during the shooting." Collin reminded Claire.

"If it were not for the nine-one-one call, we would have no information. I believe the public should be aware of the dangers of an unknown assailant who has struck twice."

"Is this a case of revenge?" Collin asked.

"Do we have a serial killer on our hands?"

"I believe the Justice Department classification of a serial killer is three or more kills over a period of time. I think we are dealing with a spree. However, you may be jumping the gun. We don't have confirmation of either man being dead."

"There has to be a good reason why the authorities are keeping the public in the dark." Claire pondered.

"They certainly have quite a list of suspects to contact."

"I know of two names that should be at the top of the list. At least just to clear them." Claire pondered.

"Our people on the ground have had a time locating Katherine Nolan, and Deilia refuses to talk to us."

"That's understandable, considering she is trying to get a law degree."

"Yeah, but if it were me, I would still want to clear my name publicly." Collin mentioned.

Katherine turned off the broadcast.

"Can you believe Claire and Collin are the only ones pressing this case? While everyone else lets yesterday's news be yesterday's news."

"Where do you think the lawyer is?"

"His name is Jansen." Katherine said.

"We know he is not dead."

"What we know is one of them should be dead, and the other should be living and enjoying his life. Especially after the loss of his wife."

"I can't believe he called you just a few days before he was shot."

"He wanted to talk to you and me."

"Was he trying to find out if I had anything to do with Sidney's attack?"

"I don't know; he sounded sincere." Katherine answered.

"Are you ready to go and talk to the detectives?"

"This will be a futile session... nevertheless."

Chapter 18

The Nolan's II

"It is a pleasure to meet both of you. I am sorry to drag you into this sordid mess." Detective Timbers said with hesitation.

"If I had it my way, I would have preferred to stay home." Katherine stated.

"We cannot overstate the necessity of this visit." Detective Timbers said, hoping not to stir a hornet's nest.

"How is law school?" Detective Gamin asked Deilia.

"It has opened my eyes to lots of potential for the practice. You can say I am developing the knowledge and skills to circumvent the miscarriage of justice." Deilia stated.

"You stated over the phone that you had some uncomfortable details that could shake up some old memories." Katherine looked at Detective Timbers.

"I am going to get straight to the point. Sidney Gaines is a person of interest in the shooting of Jansen Radford." Detective Timbers paused for effect.

"Either he shot Jansen Radford, or he didn't. You said you were going to get to the point." Deilia said with a calm voice.

"Okay, we have credible evidence that Sidney Gaines shot Jansen Radford."

"Is he in custody?" Deilia asked.

"I will tolerate your questions out of respect, but if you could allow me to drive the bus." Detective Timber's minor objection was short-lived.

"No, no, no! This is not our first rodeo. We have been down this road before, and we do not intend to travel this way again. My daughter asked if you have Sidney Gaines in custody." Katherine stated forcefully.

"We do not. We are actively searching for him." Detective Timbers answered reluctantly.

He preemptively misjudged the two women's prior encounters with Sidney Gaines.

"How does a man like that continue to elude the clutches of the law? It can't be the money, and certainly isn't the brains."

"Here we go again." Deilia stated.

"I assure you this time, he will pay." Detective Gamin said with fervor.

"Why 'cause he shot a lawyer?" Deilia asked.

"No, because it's the law." Detective Gamin treaded lightly considering how the law failed the Nolan's the first time around.

"Did Mr. Radford die?"

"The case is currently under investigation and not open for discussion. Our concern is yours and your daughter's safety."

"You think he's trying to settle old scores?" Deilia asked.

"Or maybe a new score." Detective Timbers answered.

"We have heard the news. Do you have that person in custody? Or perhaps it was Jansen Radford who attacked him? And Sidney Gaines retaliated after he disappeared from the hospital." Deilia rattled off several hypotheticals.

"That, too, is an ongoing investigation." Timbers winced for retaliation.

Timbers studied Deilia's body language. He wanted to reveal the evidence Detective Nick Carter retrieved from the session with Doctor Conway.

"How do you propose to protect us?" Katherine asked.

"We would like to offer you a safe house until we arrest Sidney Gaines." Detective Gamin offered.

Katherine looked at Deilia.

"Considering the man in question. We accept your offer. However, the safest house I know is my house." Katherine smiled.

"Do you have any leads as to Sidney Gaines's locality?" Deilia asked.

"Because there were no witnesses, he has a two-week lead on us."

"There are so many questions, but, I am certain because of the ongoing investigation. You can't answer any of my questions." Deilia looked at Detective Timbers.

"Yes, ma'am." Timbers answered the unspoken question.

"Are there any other family members that may be in danger?" Detective Gamin asked.

"There are a few cousins scattered up and down the East Coast. I really don't think he would go after them." Katherine confirmed.

"Do you think Sidney Gaines knows your current address?"

"With his money, it's possible, but my home has a privacy fence. The alarm system and cameras make it a fortress. The safest place I know." Katherine said.

"You know, Timbers, we can make this work to our advantage. If he is going to come after them, we should make it easy for him. Why not let the Nolans stay where it is comfortable and draw Sidney Gaines out?" Detective Gamin proffered.

"If you ladies don't mind being the decoys, I am game."

Detective Timbers resisted asking about the note. 'When Justice Comes Knocking.' This was the one piece of evidence that could tie Deilia to the attack on Sidney Gaines. He also tussled with the possibility that such a petite person could be the attacker.

Allusion

How Does It End?

Mind Travel A Case Study

"I know he can hear us." said Katherine distressfully. Her words reverberated off the walls of the room.

"Please give us another sign. You do not have to stay locked in there; you don't have to stay where you are. We need you." Deilia pleaded.

Katherine now heard Deilia's words echo throughout the room.

When she heard the sound effect, she knew it was a signal.

"This is the signal, but... why can I not remember?" She whispered to herself.

She watched Agent Underwood interrogate her husband.

"Maybe the Doc is right. Maybe today, I will not shut them out. I will give them a hearing." Her husband said under his breath.

"Mr. Christensen, we will compare your story with Doctor Snow's statement..."

"Dad, if you can hear me, I need you. Letting you go hurts so bad." Deilia's voice reverberated off the walls.

"Who is she talking to?" Katherine mumbled.

"If there are the slightest discrepancies, if the stories don't make sense, you will hear from me again." Agent Underwood's voice collided with the girl's voice.

"I can see how that could be fuel for the bonfire." Her husband tried to joke with Agent Underwood.

Agent Underwood stood up.

"If you leave town, or if anything else should move you one way or the other, please notify me. I am just a call away."

Agent Underwood and the girl's voice were echoing off each other like a weird dream.

"I think I saw his eyes move." Deilia cried out.

"Deilia, his eyes are closed." Katherine heard her voice echo, just like before.

"Mom, they rolled behind the eyelids." Deilia's voice now sounded like she was in a tunnel.

"Does that include an inner body experience? However, I don't think I will have time to dial the number. Tell my wife I am tired and I am going to listen to the voices this time. Tell the Doc I am going to give them a hearing. Just in case…"

Katherine watched her husband's body start to spasm. She remained frozen, even though her mind was pushing her to run to her husband's aid.

Agent Underwood finally noticed his primary audience was experiencing a seizure.

"He's fading. Get the doctor in here now!"

"Doctor, I thought I saw his eyes move." Deilia hoped with all hope.

"We removed him from the machine only thirty minutes ago. Signs of consciousness can come in many forms."

"Mom, are you sure we did the right thing?"

"Would someone do something? Don't just watch him!" Katherine said, she tried to move, but she, too, was in a catatonic state.

Katherine also heard herself speaking, but they were different words.

"It has been twenty-eight days, fourteen days longer than we agreed. We have to consider what he would want," Katherine said to Deilia.

She sniffled.

"I know that voice." Katherine heard her husband speak. However, his lips did not move. "Come on, who are these people?" He said again, but still no movement from his lips.

The people were scampering about the room.

Another agent put her cheek to her husband's face, then raised her head. She checked his pulse.

Agent Underwood wore a look of confusion on his face, certainly puzzled by the man's medical state.

The other agent shook her head from side to side.

"No, check again. He can't be gone. Somebody do something! You cannot let my husband die." Katherine shouted as she pleaded.

"Maybe we should have talked to him more." Deilia's voice echoed even louder now.

"We have talked to him every day, pleading with him, pouring our hearts out." Katherine heard her voice, and then she heard herself sobbing.

Deilia joined her.

"Who are these people?" Her husband's voice was resounding in her head, but his body lay on the floor, unresponsive to the agent's urging.

"You two should get some rest. It has been a long and stressful month for you both. If your husband has any fight left, he will certainly put forth the effort for you two," Katherine heard someone else's voice.

The group stood over the bed looking at the man.

"Come on you two, the doctors and nurses have prepared the room next door for you."

"Katherine, Deilia, please come with us. We will notify you immediately if Mr. Nolan's condition changes."

As Katherine heard voices, her surroundings started fading.

"Katherine, Deilia Nolan, wait, what is…" Katherine heard her husband's voice again.

She felt she was dreaming, a dream she did not want to leave. She struggled to remain in the moment.

She asked herself, "Why is this happening?" Then she heard her husband's words spoken so clearly. It was not like her daughter's voice or even her own, which was echoing throughout the room.

"Because I want to see how it ends."

"Just a little longer. Just let us stay thirty more minutes." Katherine heard Deilia plead.

Deilia's voice reverberated.

"If you insist." The other voice said, with a warm note in their tone. Their voices echoed as well.

Then, in an instant, Katherine was standing on the side of the road.

She saw her husband riding his bike. She was watching as he approached a hill.

Then she saw a car coming over the hill from the other direction. Its tires were not touching the pavement.

She watched motionless, helpless, and unable to yell.

The car collided with her husband and his bike.

The bike and her husband left the pavement, and then her husband's body left the motorcycle, sailing through the air.

She watched the car return to the pavement and speed away.

Katherine heard a distinct crackling sound coming from her husband's neck.

At that moment, in her mind, she fell apart, screaming and crying at the same time.

"Why, this can't be. Why is this happening?"

Again, she heard her husband's voice.

"Because I want to see how it ends."

Then there was an eerie darkness; a void

"What is going on? How did I get here?"

In the void, she heard voices.

"Guy Nolan, that is his name. He is never going to be the same."

"Poor fella. If he comes out of this, I don't think he will want to live."

"I cannot believe the person that hit him did not stick around."

"Yeah, I know. It probably would have bought him some more time."

Then there was nothing, just silence and darkness.

Then she appeared in an ambulance.

And there were voices again.

"His vitals keep going in and out."

"Get the portable defibrillator."

"But he has a Do Not Resuscitate card in his wallet."

"Has his family been notified?"

"I do not know. If you are going to do this, check his heart first."

The voices stopped; there was a brief void and then nothingness.

Then, as if someone had turned the light switch back on, there was a bright light and then darkness again.

The voices returned.

"We have a slight heartbeat! Do it!"

"We have a steady pulse now."

She witnessed what looked like a flash of lightning, followed by a parade of people she did not know.

The void returned, both unsettling and captivating. There was nothing, just the thought of existence.

The light flashed on again.

Katherine was now standing in front of a tree, watching her husband climb it. He had a coil of rope around his shoulder, with a noose dangling at the end.

She said, "Déjà vu, I have been here before, but..." she paused. "How did I get here?"

"Take me back to the beginning. Anywhere but here. At least show me how it ends."

Her husband's voice came to her again.

"Because we want to see how it ends."

"Why is she not coming out of it?" Deilia asked.

"This is her second time in, and now your father's memories have fused to hers. In effect, his memories have become hers. She is likely reliving what you yourself saw."

"The motorcycle accident, the face of the man who caused all this drama, the license plate, the tree, all of it?"

"Yes." the doctor said grievously.

"She is seeing you die over and over again Dad, that cannot be the way for her." Deilia cried.

"I know, honey."

"What are we going to do?"

"We have to wait." Doctor Conway said reassuringly. "I have to go look in on another patient. I will be back momentarily. Keep talking to her. She can hear you, and once she gets the answer she is looking for, she will find her way back to you." He smiled.

They returned the smile, but neither said anything.

"Just remember how we got here."

"Dad, she's awake."

"Welcome back." Guy said with a smile.

He was hovering at the bedside where his wife had laid for two days.

"It seemed..." she paused.

"You don't have to say anything."

"It seemed like a year passed, and then, for a few seconds, there was an empty void. Then the same scene played over again, but when I heard the crackling sound this time..." Katherine paused. "Like a ride at a carnival, I was whipped back to the room with you and Deilia." Katherine explained.

"Mom, you gave us a god-awful fright." Deilia whimpered."

"I am so glad to see you have awakened." Doctor Conway said.

"I do not want to do this again, but I do not have good news for you." Katherine turned from the doctor to her husband.

"You don't have to. We will just have to live with what we have." He already knew the answer to the lingering question that had plagued him for months.

"You need to know, there is nothing, there is no end. I tried to stay in that room, but it faded." Katherine said.

"That Agent Underwood was so callous, he, she, I couldn't tell. Just letting you die while interrogating you for something you did not do. Your sub-conscience is potent, Dad." Deilia chimed in with a note of frustration and exuberance.

"I believe Agent Underwood was a reflection of the two sides of your dad trying to work out the results of that horrible accident." Katherine suggested.

"The driver of the vehicle got off easy, but I have a sketch of his face etched in my head, the fear in his eyes." Deilia stopped.

"With the description and the license plate number, the authorities will arrest him soon." Katherine inserted.

"It is truly strange how the mind works; for the likes of me, I can neither recall seeing his face or the look in his eyes." Guy pondered.

"The mind and brain are fascinating places. Yours may be shielding you from those brief seconds. I have to check on my other patients. I will let you all continue to reminisce now that you have your wife and mother back." Doctor Conway said.

"Thank you for the work you are doing here." Guy smiled.

"My pleasure."

Doctor Conway left the room.

The sign could not have been more descriptive.
Center for Neurology and Brain Exploration
Founded by Samantha and Samuel Conway

Inside was a thriving research facility like no other. It housed a research team and patients, all aware of the goal and mission: to understand the marvel known as the brain.

A marvel of a building, it seemed to be constructed primarily of glass. The glass construction would undoubtedly account for it being one level. However, the mind's eye would give into the illusion that, it was a small facility until you took that second look. The second look would reveal a facility that must have been at least a half mile wide. Because of the width, the human eye could not determine the depth of the structure. The walkway was a mixture of stone, marble, wood, and grass.

As the sun shined on the building, it produced an image that appeared to be cloaked.

"What is next for the Nolan family?" Doctor Conway asked.

"I think we will take a nice vacation, perhaps to Hawaii. A real trip."

"Speaking of traveling, I need a vacation." Doctor Conway laughed.

There was a knock at the door.

Doctor Conway made his way to the door and opened it.

"The girl is awake, and the rest of the family is ready for you."

"I will be right there."

Doctor Conway turned to Guy, Katherine, and Deilia Nolan.

"Send me a postcard."

How You Got Here

You have taken a wild ride. This psychological thriller originally started with Killing Myself. I am ecstatic to continue this series and can't wait to see how it develops.

It would be a considerable theft to explain the dynamics of this tantalizing adventure. Therefore, you get to experience the revelations experienced by the characters, thus allowing you to arrive at the same conclusion the traveler reaches.

Traversing Minds allows the reader to enter a world not defined by time or space in this realm. There are no limitations or rules but one: tread lightly! Enjoy the trip.

Traversing Minds

Starts Here

About the Author

Arthur is originally from Culpeper, Virginia. However, he has decided that Heathsville, Virginia is the perfect place to nurture his passion for writing. He has written, illustrated, and animated five children's books, and has also explored writing short stories, novellas, and informational material. In 2021, he released his first novel, The Umbrella Clause, which allowed him to fully embrace his identity as a writer and storyteller.

Arthur has been a business manager, an IT professional, and an accidental librarian. His knack for quickly understanding new subjects gives him a unique ability to excel in any profession he chooses. A long-time curator from New York once described him as a polymath because of his broad knowledge across various topics. Given his wealth of experience and vivid imagination, Arthur is sure to create some of the most thrilling stories yet to come.

Thank You